A FROZEN S.

HAUNTING AVERY WINTER BOOK
BOOK IV

DIONNE LISTER

Copyright © 2022 by Dionne Lister

Imprint: Dionne Lister

Sydney, Australia

Contact: dionnelisterauthor@gmail.com

ISBN 978-1-922407-34-4

Paperback edition

Cover art by Robert Baird

Editing by Hot Tree Editing

Proofreading L. Brodey

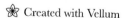 Created with Vellum

I don't often do these any more because I've written so many books, I'm running out of people to thank, BUT in this case, I need to thank two special people. To Becky, my editor, you always shuffle like crazy to accommodate my lateness, and I appreciate it more than you know. Without you, my books wouldn't be as good as they are. And to LB, one of my very best friends who also proofreads for me, and this time it was on such short notice and done quickly because I'm in a hurry. Thank you so much for doing everything you could to help me. Love you, ladies xx.

CHAPTER 1

So much for waking up early on Monday to be ready for another work week. I'd returned from my jog to find I was out of coffee grounds. Such an unacceptable situation. Which was why I was standing outside the village supermarket waiting for it to open at seven. I checked my phone. 6:58 a.m. The next two minutes were probably going to take forever.

I gazed around. What. In. Hades? Three shops down, a middle-aged man in super-short running shorts and a singlet top stood facing the butchers. I wished I was mistaken, but I wasn't. He was urinating on the footpath, some of the droplets flicking up to hit the shop window. Ben Greaves, the owner of Manesbury Meaty Morsels, wouldn't be too happy about that. Since he wasn't here to see it, I'd have to intervene.

"Hey, you can't do that!"

The man jerked around to look at me... without putting anything away. Urine sprayed everywhere like an out-of-control hose, and I shut my eyes. *Eye bleach. Someone give me eye bleach.*

"What's it to you, missy? Ain't none of your business."

Hoping he'd made himself decent, I opened my eyes. Hope was

for suckers, apparently. "Yes it is. You can't just go to the toilet wher-ever you feel like it. This is a public place."

A voice came from behind me. "What in the dickens is wrong with you, weirdo?" The voice taunting me was one I knew. Oh joy… less. It was at that moment I noticed a woman across the street staring at me. My cheeks heated. Bloody ghosts. How was I supposed to tell the difference when they didn't look dissimilar to living people? I turned to face Joyless who was chewing gum and peering at me as if I were crazy. Great. Just great.

"I'm practicing for a play I'm in. What's it to you?"

She raised her brows. "Ha, yeah right." She leaned towards me, eyes narrowed into judgemental slits. "You're a freaking nutter. I knew there was something off about you."

I shrugged, doing my best to pretend I didn't care. At least I didn't care what she thought, but what she might tell other people wasn't going to be good. The last thing I needed was my friends asking me what I was doing, yelling at nobody in the street. Cripes, what if it got back to Mr Macpherson? He was already on alert because of my darling mother. "You've obviously never acted before." I gave her a smug look. And when was the supermarket going to open? It must be seven by now.

One side of Joyless's top lip hitched up in a disbelieving sneer. "What has that got to do with anything?"

I rolled my eyes, as if to say "oh my God, how stupid can you be?" "It's a common method actors use to get over stage fright. Practicing lines in public is a great way to overcome performance nerves." I gave her a fake smile, and when the door rattled as Vanessa—the supermarket manager—unlocked it, I held back a relieved breath. If I'd needed coffee before, I doubly needed it now. It was the only thing that would save my morning.

Joyless glared at me and whisper hissed, "I'm going to tell Finny how crazy you are. It's about time he saw what I saw." The door opened, and she bumped me out of the way with her shoulder as she barged past. I resisted the urge to hurry after her and kick one foot into the other. It would be satisfying to trip her over, but knowing how much she disliked me, she'd be sure to have me charged. It wasn't worth it. One day Karma would trip her for me. At least I hoped so. Also, what did Finnegan have to do with anything? Hmm, she was probably sweet on him—and who could blame her? I smiled. She'd just given me fodder for annoying her in the future. Yay for small victories.

"You're in early." Vanessa was in her mid-thirties, but with the dark circles under her eyes and a smattering of greys in her long brown hair, she looked older. Having twin three-year-olds and working a full-time job would do that to a person.

I brushed off the lingering bad vibes from Joyless and smiled. "I'm out of coffee grounds, and I won't survive without my morning coffee."

She returned my smile. "You're in luck. We've got a special on coffee this week—30 per cent off."

"Ooh, it's my lucky day!" I grinned. My morning had just turned around.

She passed me a handbasket from the stacked tower next to her. "Have fun."

"Ha, thanks." I made my way straight to the coffee aisle. Sure enough, orange labels hung under each section of products. My favourite coffee was discounted, so I grabbed two large packets. Score! Because I'd saved some money, it meant I could grab my favourite chocolate-fudge ice cream.

I wandered to the far end of the store where rows of fridges lined the aisle. I was about a third of the way along when a tall, beefy guy with no neck—probably in his late twenties—stood in front of me. "Hey, sweetie. I need some help. Now!"

Sweetie? I was about to say I was no one's sweetie, except the small golden-coloured trophy sticking out of his eye, together with the blood smeared on his face, clued me into the fact that he probably wasn't alive. My head fell back, and I stared at the ceiling. Argh, so much for my day improving. I blew out an irritated breath and lowered my chin until I was meeting his worried gaze. "Where are you?"

His forehead wrinkled. "I'm here, but I'm also…" He turned his head to look at the door which interrupted the row of fridges midway along the wall. "Um, I'm in the cold storage." He scratched his head. "Am I dead?"

"I'd say so. It looks like someone stabbed you in the eye with a trophy of some sort." I leaned forward to get a better look. I could see about three-quarters of it with the rest embedded in the guy's eye. It was a person with some kind of football boots and shorts on. One arm was by its side; the other must be holding something up. So, a sporting trophy. Hmm, the plaque on the bottom was covered in blood, but I was sure I could make out the word "Rugby." "It might have gone through to your brain." He didn't appear to have any other injuries, but then again, I couldn't see his back. "Can you lead the way to the cold storage?"

He turned, and so did my stomach. There it was—a knife sticking out of his back and a lot more blood all over his sky-blue polo shirt and tan trousers. I didn't want to alarm him since he was still coming to terms with being dead, so I said nothing as I followed him. He held his hand out to push the clouded-plastic door open, but he went straight through. Surely that had clued him in the first time. Maybe he wasn't ready to accept things just yet. Every other ghost I'd come across had been dead for at least a few hours. Did that mean he'd been killed in the last hour or so?

Holding my breath, anticipating what I might find, I pushed the door open and stopped just inside it. The ghost stood next to his large body, which lay face down next to a ladder, his face turned towards me, the eye socket a mushy red hole. A pile of boxes and crates of milk yet to be unpacked sat against the wall next to the bloody scene. "Were you sorting the deliveries when you were killed?"

He looked at me. "Yeah." He scratched the side of his head again. "So, do you think you could call an ambulance or something? I haven't got all day. I've got rugby practice at twelve." That explained the lack of neck.

My forehead tightened. Softening things wasn't going to help him if he was in denial. I'd have to use the Band-Aid method. "Um, no. I'm sorry, but your body isn't coming back. This is rather final. Do you know who killed you?" I didn't want to waste time. I should call the police right now. They probably had me on one of the aisle security cameras entering this room, which was off limits to shoppers. I glanced around. Luckily, I couldn't see any cameras in here. Maybe they respected their employees' privacy, or maybe it was just well hidden.

Panic emanated from his gaze, and he shook his head, as if denying the situation could change it. "But I can't be dead. I'm only twenty-eight. This can't be happening." This time, instead of scratching his head, he grabbed a fistful of his dark hair and yanked.

I pulled my phone out and dialled nine, nine, nine. "Hello, I'd like to report a murder." Reporting the discovery of dead bodies was becoming a bad habit.

When I got off the phone with the dispatcher, I took a quick shot of the body and the room. There was a small window on the back wall and a door. Both were closed. Interestingly, there was no trophy sticking out of the body's eye, and there was none that I could see anywhere, yet his ghost still sported the gruesome attachment. Hmm. This was the first time I'd seen something on a spirit that wasn't there in person.

I had to start my investigation somewhere and was about to ask him his name when the hiss of the plastic door scraping against the floor made me turn.

Joyless stood there, a look of triumph on her face, as if she'd caught me doing something abhorrent, because sneaking into a forbidden supermarket room was the height of law breaking. Her satisfaction didn't last long though. She spied the body lying in a pool of blood behind me, and her face went white. Her mouth hinged open, and I covered my ears.

Then came her almighty scream.

CHAPTER 2

When the police arrived, Bellamy sent me to wait out in the aisle. By this time, the ghost had disappeared, and Joyless was sitting on a chair the store manager had procured. We waited next to the ice cream display. Once all this was done, I was going to grab a tub of chocolate fudge and nut, pay for my purchases, and go home. This was too much drama before I'd had any coffee.

Some colour had returned to Joyless's face, and it seemed she'd overcome her shock, if the glare she shot my way was any indication. "What did you do to that guy?"

I gave her a "you've got to be kidding" look. "You do realise that if I'd killed him, I'd have blood all over me. And why would I kill him? I don't even know him."

She folded her arms. "You're a psychopath. You're always finding dead bodies. How many is that now since you've been here?" She stared at her hand as she popped each finger straight, one by one. She finally managed to count to four. Her head jerked up, and her narrowed gaze found mine. "Four! Funny how no one got murdered before you showed up. I bet you're like those rogue firemen who start fires just so they can put them out and be heroes.

You kill people and"—she made air quotes with both hands—"*solve* the murders. Everyone thinks you're smart, but I know you're a fraud and a killer."

If I thought anyone would take her seriously, I'd be worried, but they wouldn't. My tone was light, and my face relaxed. "Do you ever wonder how killers choose their victims? I bet it's the people who annoy them the most." I smiled.

Her eyes widened, and she slid her chair backwards, away from me. "You're a crazy b—"

Bellamy came through the door from the coolroom and looked at me, then Joyless. "I'd like to speak to both of you separately. Are you up for it?"

Joyless stood and pointed at me. "She did it, Sergeant. I saw her in there with the body. That woman's a murderer. I saw her talking to herself before she went in. She's totally loopy." She pointed her finger at her head and made numerous circular motions around her ear. What were we, five?

I rolled my eyes. I should introduce her to my parents and Brad —they'd all hit it off for sure.

Bellamy turned his critical gaze on me, sweeping down my body and back up again. His mouth tilted up ever so slightly on one corner before he got himself under control. "You don't seem to be covered in blood, so I'll assume your innocence for now." His back was to Joyless, and he actually winked at me.

I smiled. "Thanks, Sergeant. You have no idea how much I appreciate that assumption."

He turned back to Joyless. "Constable Percy will interview you shortly. Do you mind waiting for another five minutes?"

She tilted her chin up in a haughty expression. "Fine, but I hope you put her in gaol. She's a danger to this community."

To his credit, he said nothing before turning back to me. "Let's have this conversation in my car."

"Can I pay for my groceries first?"

He blinked.

"I'm out of coffee, which is why I was here in the first place." Maybe a normal person would be thrown by finding a dead body, but in my bizarre world, it was a common occurrence. If I was going to have a meltdown every time this happened, I'd be spending most of my days in hysterics. It was better to just get on with things.

He nodded. "I understand."

"Thanks." I bit back a grin—there was a dead body in the next room after all—but I let the satisfaction of having someone on my side warm my heart. At least I wasn't a stranger here now, and normal people who weren't vindictive realised I wasn't a terrible person. I grabbed the ice cream from the freezer and added it to my basket, then went to the register.

Vanessa stood at a register, having replaced another younger employee who was crying near the front door. A policeman was talking quietly to her. Vanessa glanced at the woman, then back to me. "She really liked Adam. They'd been on a couple of dates."

"Oh, that's sad. I hope she's okay."

Vanessa eyed Bellamy who was waiting for me just outside the front doors. She lowered her voice. "He was a good enough worker, but he was a bit of a pig. It's annoying that I have to find someone else to fill his position, and I feel for his family, but I wasn't a fan. If it had been up to me, I would've fired him a while ago, but the owner is a friend of his family's."

"Oh, wow. How long had he worked here?"

"About four months."

Bellamy stuck his head through the door. "Are you coming, Winters, or are you having a chat? I haven't got all day."

I figured it was a rhetorical question, so I put my three items on the conveyer belt. "Yikes. Time to go, I guess."

Vanessa rung the items up, put them in a plastic bag, and I paid. Hopefully the interview wouldn't take too long because my yummy ice cream would melt, and it hadn't been on sale.

As soon as I stepped outside, Bellamy pivoted and walked to his car, which was parked across the road. "You can sit in the front." He opened his own door and got in. I went around the other side and did the same. When I'd shut the door, he took out his notepad and pen. "Begin at the beginning."

A burst of adrenaline fired through me. Bloody Joyless had been a distraction, and now I didn't have my story straight. I hoped my brain could come up with a believable lie on short notice. I explained everything up to the point the ghost had asked me to follow him. "Well, I couldn't find the ice cream I wanted, and I knew there was another cold storage area. No one else was around to ask, so I wandered in there myself... which might have been a mistake. It was a horrible surprise." He nodded. *Yay, brain! Thanks for not letting me down.*

He cleared his throat. "I bet. You do, as Miss Stick pointed out, have a penchant for finding dead bodies. You're like some kind of macabre divining rod."

I stifled a giggle at Joyless's last name—Stick... Joy Stick. Maybe I was immature, but it was hilarious. Maybe her parents weren't much better than mine. Satisfied that I'd staved off my laughter, I placed a palm on my chest. "Why thank you, kind sir. No one's ever called me macabre before. It's such a compliment."

He gave me a "look." "You know what I mean." He wrote something down. "Have you ever seen the deceased before?"

"Nope."

"Are you sure?"

"Positive. Vanessa said his name is Adam."

"Yes, Adam Murphy. He plays rugby for Cramptonbury." So, that definitely was the word "rugby" on that trophy. It was a shame I couldn't mention anything to Bellamy. This was a massive clue. "He's a bit of a legend in rugby circles. He played for the Exeter Chiefs for two seasons. Then he had a two-month stint in the England side. An injury put him out, and he never made it back to that level. That was about four years ago."

"So, his dream was professional rugby?"

"Yes. He did well to bounce back from his disappointments. It's a damn shame it's ended like this for him."

"How did he end up stacking shelves at a supermarket?"

Bellamy stared at me, possibly weighing up how much to tell me, if anything at all. "He did averagely at his studies because rugby was his goal. But a lad has to earn money somehow." He cocked his head to the side. "Now, I'm the one who's supposed to be asking you questions."

I smiled. "Police aren't the only ones who like to ask questions, you know."

His lips twitched. "Apparently." He asked me a few more questions, and then we were done. "If you think of anything else, let me know."

"Okay, will do." I opened the door. "And if *you* need any help, let *me* know." I grinned.

He raised his brows. "Have a good day, Winters." Typical. He was never going to make this easy for me.

I hopped out of the car and crossed the road. It was time to go home and drink my hard-won coffee.

CHAPTER 3

I arrived at work a little after ten thirty and my interview with the local hairdresser owner, Verity. The salon was having a special on cuts and blow dries. The interview should've taken no more than ten minutes, but everyone wanted to talk about the murder, and, of course, they all knew I'd found the body. One of the young hairdressers had the cojones to ask if I'd done it. Seriously. Would I be wandering around if the police thought I had? Looked like Miss Stick had managed to set the village grapevine on fire. I smirked just thinking about Joystick. It didn't hurt to act like a five-year-old every now and then.

Carina and Finnegan were at their desks. They both looked up when I stepped into the room. Carina stood and hurried over. "Love! What happened? Is it true you found ano'der body?"

I shrugged. "Yes. I'm surprised Vinegar hasn't confirmed it with Sergeant Bellamy."

He held his hands palms up. "What can I say? I've been busy."

Carina smirked. "He tried calling Bellamy, but he didn't answer."

I chuckled. "Busted."

His mouth dropped open. "No need to be rude."

I wrinkled my brow. "What?" Then it hit me, and I laughed. "Busted." I spelled it out. "Not the spelling with an *a r*."

Carina laughed. "I'd ask if you were okay, but after everyt'ing d'at happened at Donigal's farm, I know you can handle it."

"Thanks. It wasn't pretty though. Especially before having my coffee, and considering that Joyless was there to blame me for it." I couldn't be sure, but that tightening around Finnegan's eyes could've been a tiny flinch. I put my stuff on my desk and then my hands on my hips. "She told you, didn't she?"

He tapped a pointer finger on the table for a few beats. "Yes. She called me just after she spoke to the police interviewer."

Carina rolled her eyes. "Of course she did. She's been trying to date you again. She's got it bad. Why not try and drum up a bit of sympat'y?" She looked at me and smirked. "But she didn't get what she wanted. Finn told her he was too busy to see her and asked if she wanted him to send her sister to the cafe."

I couldn't help grinning. "Too funny. Having said that, I do feel a bit sorry for her. It's not every day that she sees dead bodies, so she would legit be stressed out. Although, she didn't have to follow me in there, hoping to catch me out at who knows what. And then telling everyone I did it." I shook my head. "She's an inferior human."

Carina chuckled. "Ooh, I like d'at. She definitely is an inferior human."

I went around to the other side of my desk and sat. "It's time I wrote up my experience from this morning." I looked across at Finnegan. "You haven't written anything yet, have you?"

"No. You're in luck. I'm writing an in-depth article about political sabotage in Exeter council. I've been gathering research for the past three months. This one will take me a good three or four days to get right. There'll be a few drafts before it'll be publishable. Besides, the least I can do for you after the morning you've had is let you get an easy piece out of it." His mouth lifted on one side in a cute half smile. I sighed internally at his hotness. One day I'd work out how to ignore the effect he had on me. Today was not that day, unfortunately. At least I managed to keep my sighing on the inside.

"Thanks. I appreciate it." I was about to ask if they knew the deceased, but that might be pushing it too far—getting the article *and* using their intel. Besides, even though the conversation at the hairdresser had included me being grilled about being a killer, I'd managed to find out more about Adam. I had enough to write a short article. Of course, I wanted to write about who killed him, so I was going to visit his rugby club later. Adam's ghost had said the team had training at twelve, and I was going to be there.

❦

Cramptonbury sporting complex—which housed three rugby fields, four tennis courts, a basketball court, and a clubhouse—was situated on the far side of Cramptonbury, on the way out of town. All the tennis courts were occupied by well-groomed women who wore the latest tennis fashions. Ah, to be a lady of leisure. What would that be like, never having to do anything you didn't want to? Not that I disliked my job. In fact, I loved my job, except when I had to witness men kissing trees, and, of course, finding dead bodies wasn't my favourite pastime, but the job couldn't really be blamed for that. The lightning strike could take all the credit.

The two-storey brick clubhouse sat between the fields and the courts. I made my way over, pen and notebook in hand, my handbag slung over my shoulder. The more official I looked, the better. I stopped and took a photo of the plaque over the clubhouse door—it would be a good inclusion in my piece. As far as getting a picture of Adam was concerned, if I could get his parents to agree to something, I'd use that, and if I couldn't, I'd use one sourced from the media, and just get permission from whoever posted it in the first place. If he'd been a reasonably successful sportsman, there would be images of him out there.

Instead of going inside the clubhouse, I walked around to the rear and the rugby fields. I'd turned up at twelve twenty—I wanted to make sure they'd had time to find out the news and speak to each other.

Half of the young men on the field ran drills around cones, the other half jogged in a line, passing the ball back and forth, whoever had the ball accelerating to put themselves in front of the receiver—forward passes were a no-no. I'd played my share of Oztag in Australia, and whilst it wasn't identical to rugby, it followed many of the same principles.

I approached the two men who stood on the sideline observing the action. The sharp scent of cut grass intertwined with damp soil, taking me back to summers at home when I was a kid, running under the sprinkler with my sister and neighbourhood friends. The melancholy that hit me wasn't because I missed those days—it was because I realised that the happy memories were few and far between, and none of them contained my parents. Surely it hadn't been that bad? Was I only remembering what suited my current narrative? One of the men watching shouted something to the players, and it brought me back to the present.

The taller of the men looked to be about six foot and in his thirties. The shorter one was only slightly taller than me. I pegged him to be in his fifties and an ex-player—the lack of neck was a dead giveaway, but the slight paunch suggested that he didn't play regularly any more, if ever. I assumed them to be the coaches, genius that I was.

The older one was the first to notice me, and by the lecherous look in his eyes, he'd be my first target. He was already interested... maybe not in what I had to say, but hopefully he'd be keen to impress me. Here went nothing. I tempered my smile to something polite and not overly happy since they'd just lost one of their team members. "Hi, I'm Avery Winters, and I'm doing a short piece on Adam for the *Manesbury Daily*. I'm sorry for your loss, and I know this probably isn't the best time, but would you be able to give me some information for my article? He was rather a big deal to many of our residents." Maybe a bit of flattery of their mate would make them feel more important.

Line cast, and I didn't have to wait long. The older guy licked his bottom lip and held out his hand. "Tom Whitely, assistant coach. Pleased to meet you, Avery. I'd be happy to answer any questions."

The younger man looked at me, his hazel eyes not so enamoured. "I'm sorry, but we're in the middle of training. Come back in an hour." He flicked his gaze back to the field, a dismissal if ever I'd seen one.

Waiting for an hour wasn't the end of the world, and maybe that wasn't such a bad idea anyway. Although, I'd seen this ploy before—tell the reporter you'll speak to them later, and when later comes, they've either disappeared or have to rush off. I smiled properly this time—I wasn't taking no for an answer. "Okay, sure. It'll be good to speak to his teammates too. I'm sure they'll have a lot to say."

I saw the younger guy's jaw bunch. Someone didn't want me speaking to the players, which was weird. He turned his head and gave his assistant coach a nod. The older man grinned at me. "Why don't we have a quick word over there, then." He nodded at a bench seat concreted into the ground. "I'd hate for you to have to hang around—you're probably a very busy girl."

My eyebrows jumped up of their own accord. *Girl.*

He put his hand on my lower back and gave a slight push. My heart thudded faster, and I swallowed the urge to yell "get your hand off me." I stepped to the side, and his hand lost contact. Powerwalking seemed appropriate—a fast-moving target was harder to touch. When I reached the seat, I sat to one side of the middle but left another bottom's worth of space on my other side. I figured if he wanted to sit close to me and I was on the end of the seat, I'd have nowhere to go. Stupid stuff we women had to think about sometimes. And maybe I was overreacting, but I'd been in enough situations to know it was a possibility, and it was always better to be prepared.

Surprisingly, he sat not quite in the middle, but a bit further out towards the other end of the chair, leaving a few inches between us. It wasn't great, but our legs weren't touching, so it was a start. "Sorry about Toby. He's upset. It's come as quite a shock."

"I can understand." It was a shock to me, too, but I wasn't going to mention that. I poised my pen over my notebook. "What position did he play?"

"Fly-half. He's also the captain." His gaze shifted to the men on the field. "They're going to be lost without him for a bit. This isn't good for the team." His eyes found mine again. "Best player we had. The lads are going to miss him."

I wrote down what he'd said and made an additional note for myself—team members unlikely to be the killers. No one liked losing, and from what their assistant coach was saying, it was probably going to come to that without their star player. "That's sad. I bet the fans will be devastated too."

He chuckled. "Yeah, especially the women. They flocked to him like flies to sh—" He clamped his lips closed. "Sorry about that. Don't quote me on that bit."

"Don't worry. My editor wouldn't appreciate it either." I blinked. It wasn't my imagination. While we'd been talking, he'd surreptitiously slid closer to me. Our thighs weren't even an inch apart. My gut was always right. I looked over at the players. "They sure train hard."

He took the bait and stared at the team. "They do." By the time he'd turned back, I'd shifted a few inches away. Even if he kept it up, the interview wouldn't last long enough for me to fall off the end. I'd make sure of it. "Do you have anyone to replace him on such short notice?"

He scratched his chin. "There's a couple of younger ones in our premier division that look good to come up. Another one of the boys on the team will become captain. But no one's as good as Adam."

"Was he married or seeing anyone? It would be good to mention them in the article if he was. If I can avoid speaking to his parents, I will. I don't want to upset them."

He looked over at the other coach, then back at me. "Cath Daily. They lived together for the past two years, but, and don't mention this, he had girls on the side." He smiled. "That lad could pull 'em, God rest his soul. Two or three at once sometimes. He was the envy of us all." Gross. He sounded like a total tosspot. Maybe I didn't want to cover this murder after all. At this point, his personality was so off-putting that I didn't care who killed him. Did that make me a bad person? Meh. Whatever.

I bit my tongue, literally. I was representing the *Manesbury Daily*, and the last thing I needed was someone complaining about me being disrespectful.

A tall, lean, broad-shouldered young man, maybe even a teenager, ran towards us from the clubhouse. "Who's that?" Changing the subject seemed like a good option. I'd had enough of talking about Adam and his disrespect for his girlfriend. Not to mention, the culture of the whole club seemed distasteful… at least to me. They really needed to get with the times.

He stared at the young man and chuckled. "That's Byron. He does odd jobs for the club and plays at a lower club level. He's a great player, but he hasn't filled out properly yet. He's a nice enough kid."

"How old is he?"

"Eighteen. We pick a couple of kids a year from the lower grades. They like being recognised and hanging with the good players. Makes them feel more important. If they don't get a position, we turn them over within two years. The older they get, the less pliable they are." Wow, this guy was awesome, and by awesome, I meant a pig.

"Do they get paid?"

He laughed. "Of course not. It's voluntary. Besides they get prestige amongst their mates."

The head coach turned and stared at us as Byron finally reached us. I hoped Byron got out before Tom made him not so nice. "Coach Whitely, Mr Potter's on the phone."

Tom jumped up. Mr Potter must be important. "Right you are. I'll be there in a moment." He turned to me. "Nice to meet you, Avery. If you need to speak to me in the future, you can ring the club phone. I'll always be happy to talk to you." He held out his hand.

I summoned a limp smile and shook his hand. "Great. Thanks."

The head coach was still glaring at us, and Byron was shifting from foot to foot. It had been obvious from the start that I wasn't welcome. But that was fine with me. This was one club I was happy not to be part of. But even though the head coach wanted me gone,

Tom hadn't received the memo. I resisted the urge to shudder under his persistent stare.

"Coach?" Byron's forehead wrinkled. Seemed he might be as uncomfortable about Tom staring at me as I was.

Tom smiled. "Call me sometime, and we'll go out to dinner." He winked, and Byron cringed. *I'm with you there, buddy.*

I'd always prided myself on my ability to be polite and professional under most circumstances. But sometimes you had to throw your standards out the window.

"I don't think so. You're old enough to be my father. And correct me if I'm wrong, but isn't that a wedding ring on your finger?" His answer was irrelevant, so I turned and walked off, leaving Tom with his mouth gaping and Byron fighting a grin.

It was lucky I didn't want to pursue this case because I'd likely never get their cooperation again. I grinned. Ill-advised or not, burning a bridge had never been so freaking satisfying. I gave it five out of five stars.

CHAPTER 4

L ate in the afternoon, I was about to leave the office—Finnegan was already gone, and Carina was packing her bag—when Mr Macpherson strode in. He gave Carina a nod. "Kelly."

She stood and returned the nod. "Julian."

His gaze jerked to me. "Winters, just the person I wanted to see."

Hmm, had Tom complained? "What can I help you with, Julian?" It was still weird to call him by his first name. And why did I have to call him Julian when he called me Winters?

"We've published your article on Adam's murder. I wanted you to know that it was okay, but I've added to it. I feel you were a bit sparse with some of his accomplishments and what he meant to this community. He was a talented player, respected by many."

"Player" was the word all right. "Oh, okay. Sorry I didn't do a great job." Hashtag *SorryNotSorry*, as they said on social media.

He waved his hand as if to say, don't worry about it. "Give it a read anyway, just so you know where you can improve."

"Of course."

He stepped through the door, then stopped and turned. He

grabbed the doorframe and tapped it a few times. "Oh, and I have another assignment for you that needs to be covered tomorrow. Just check your inbox when you get home and make the arrangements."

I smiled. "Will do."

"Good-oh." I blinked, and he was already gone. If Carina hadn't acknowledged him, I might've thought he was a ghost.

As I packed up my stuff, Carina grabbed her things and came to my desk. She looked down at me. "Don't worry about it. Every now and d'en he'll add somet'ing to one of d'e articles. He probably wants to look good to the bigwigs in Exeter. Adam's uncle is the mayor, Torin Murphy. If he printed something less d'an glowing, he'd hear about it. Politics, don't you know." She rolled her eyes.

I chuckled. "Yes. One of the pitfalls of our job. Thanks for caring."

She grinned. "Always, my love. See you tomorrow."

"Bye." I grabbed my backpack and wasn't far behind Carina. At least the clouds hadn't produced rain—the walk home would be pleasant, and I had my ice cream to eat when I got there. Yum. If finding a dead body was the price to pay for coffee and ice cream, so be it. I giggled to myself. I'd have to add that to the list of things I never thought I'd say.

As I reached the supermarket, I walked through a patch of icy air. I shivered. Adam materialised a few feet in front of me. The trophy, at least, was gone from his eye. He must've figured out how to change the way he appeared. "Hey, you're the blonde chick who found my body. I've been waiting for you." He looked much the same as yesterday, but he'd managed to ditch the trophy protruding from his eye.

I kept walking. My stomach muscles tensed as I braced to walk through him. Ew, it was as yuck as I thought it would be. Goosebumps peppered my arms and the hairs on the back of my neck jumped up. I didn't want to talk to him. Maybe he hadn't worked out how to leave the place he was killed, and if I kept going, I'd lose him.

"Hey! Don't ignore me, sugar. Did I do something wrong? You can see me, can't you?" His voice stayed close behind. Argh. Looked like he'd figured things out. But he didn't know for sure I could still see him, so I ignored him and kept walking at the same pace. "You looked at my face when I was in front of you. I know you can still see me. You have a hot arse." He overtook me and turned, hurrying backwards, so he could face me as I walked.

Poop. I pulled out my phone and put it to my ear because I was not going to get accused of being crazy twice in the same day. "Okay, I can still see you, but I don't want to. Please leave me alone." I hadn't asked any ghosts to leave me alone before. Could I control who spoke to me, or was it like it was with normal people?

"Aw, don't be like that." He pouted. "I just need your help. Come on; any woman would kill to help me. They fell all over themselves to hang out with me when I was alive." His shoulders sagged. There's no doubt it would be sobering to know you were dead. How long would it take for it to sink in and not be a horrific surprise every time you realised? "The things I could've done to you." He licked his lips, and I gagged.

I hoped my glare was obvious enough. "Stop being disgusting."

He smirked. "Aw, sweetie, I'm only joking. Can't a bloke have a bit of fun? Are you one of them stuck-up chicks?"

Argh, it wasn't worth arguing with him. He was never going to understand and start being a decent person. If he wasn't going to give two possum poos about my feelings, I had no compunction about hurting his... not that it was possible. "Look, you're dead. No one can help you now." If I wanted him gone, I'd have to slam that door and not give him time to jam his foot in it.

"Whoa, harsh." He grinned. "Feisty, aren't you." I ignored him, which, apparently, was an invitation for him to keep talking. Why did I forget my earbuds today? Never again. "Obviously I'm dead. I get it. But the person who killed me is out there. It's probably a serial killer, and you have to stop them. What if they kill my team-mates one by one?"

Was he conning me with this? "Why would you think it's a serial killer?" *Do not get sucked in, Avery.*

"If you agree to help me, I'll tell you." He backwards walked through a small bush, which I dodged. Damn that he was a ghost and not a real person. I would've liked to have seen him trip over.

I turned left up the laneway to home. At least once I got there, I could shut the door, and he wouldn't be able to intrude. "I don't really care. Serial killer, shmiller. I guess we'll find out soon enough if one is on the loose."

It was at that point that he must've realised I wasn't pretending to be immune to his charms. I really was, and I wasn't going to help him. He scowled. "You're a cold-hearted cow; you know that?"

Anger prickled my tongue, but I said nothing. I took a deep, calming breath and walked faster. Gone were the days when I put up with bullying from my ex and my parents, and damned if I was going to take it from a ghost.

He was no longer in front of me but hurrying along beside me and facing the right way. "Fine, then. I received a handwritten note under the windscreen wiper of my car one night. It said that they were going to kill me and come after everyone on my team."

I'd reached my front fence. I stopped and faced away from the house. I wouldn't put it past Mrs Crabby to be able to lipread. My voice was an angry whisper. I still didn't believe him, but against my better judgement, I'd give him the benefit of the doubt. Plus, my stupid journalist tendencies demanded I find out. Argh. "Do you know who it was from? Did you tell anyone?"

He smiled, triumphant. "I knew you'd come around." I gave him a "you've got to be kidding" look. He didn't miss a beat though. "I have my suspicions, and I told a couple of my mates, but I didn't want to tell the club because they take that stuff seriously, and they'd have restricted things like going to the pub, plus, well, the police."

"What about the police?"

He shrugged. "I don't know."

I rubbed my forehead. He was hiding something, and I didn't need my communications degree to know it. "Can you tell me who you think wrote the note?"

He sucked in a breath, even though he didn't need to, but then snapped his mouth shut. Why would he protect the person? Gah, I didn't need this ridiculousness. I still had to call someone about an interview tomorrow, and my ice cream was waiting.

"Look, I don't have time for this. Please go away and don't come back." I turned, opened my gate, and wasted no time unlocking the door. The idiot swore at me. Seriously? That wasn't how you convinced someone to help? When I felt like someone deserved my assistance, I gave it willingly. This guy couldn't deserve it any less.

I stepped inside and shut the door behind me. And that was the end of that as far as I was concerned.

Only, of course, it wasn't.

CHAPTER 5

When I left for work the next morning, Adam was waiting for me outside the front gate. He didn't apologise for insulting me, just went on and on about how he was important, and I should help him. Luckily, I was using my car to get to this morning's interview, and I could shut him out. It was a ten-minute drive to interview the owner of a local museum—Cramptonbury Curated Curious Curiosities. Yes, you read that correctly. Chances were, this was going to be an "interesting" visit.

The place was on the other side of Cramptonbury and halfway to the next town. I pulled into the gravel parking lot and drove past the sentry, which happened to be a person-sized, shiny, black dung beetle. Okay, so I was curious (maybe the name *was* a stroke of genius)—was this a museum full of insects or poo-themed displays? With my luck this week, it would be the latter. Hopefully, scent wouldn't be part of the experience.

There were a couple of cars in the car park. I had questions already. How did they make money if it was this quiet during the week? Did they host school excursions? What was the beetle made of? I gathered my stuff and got out of the car.

The front doors formed the mouth in a giant face. It reminded me of Luna Park in Sydney, although this face wasn't anywhere near as nightmarish. Why they had to add an element of creepiness to a place that was supposed to be fun, I couldn't work out. Seeing dead people wasn't nearly as scary as standing in front of the murdering-clown Luna Park face with its crazy eyes, rosy cheeks, and white teeth.

The front desk was unmanned. Entry, according to the sign, was five pounds. Whether or not that was a bargain was yet to be ascertained. I figured since I was there to help sell the place, I wouldn't have to pay. Maybe I'd make a donation before I left, depending on how nice the owner was.

I was five minutes early for the interview, so I thought I'd have a wander by myself. The ground floor of the two-storey building was packed with displays. They ringed the walls and filled the middle of the room, leaving a three-person-sized aisle on each side. I started on my left.

Half of a brown brick sat in a glass case. The label read, *Brick from a 1940s bungalow in Liverpool. Collected after the house was destroyed by fire.* I took a photo of it… not for the article, but so I could regale my friends with tales of my interesting day later. They were sure to take pity on me. I moved to the next display. What in Hades? I bit my lip because I wasn't sure whether to laugh or not. Was I horrified? Yes. Was it funny? Still yes. A pair of dentures sat on a white plate. This one wasn't under glass. Maybe they figured no one would want to touch it. They would be right. *Click.* Carina and Meg were going to get a kick out of this. *Aunt Mavis's dentures c1988.* Was this the guy's aunt, or was it a random aunt? At this rate, I'd have a gazillion questions for the owner, and I'd be here all day.

The next one was under glass. A grey piece of palm-sized fluff with a couple of larger bits in it. *Dust bunny, Kensington Palace c. 1985.* Throbbing began behind my eye. Was that a headache setting in or a brain aneurysm?

Before I could view the next riveting object, an older man walked up to me. He wore a green vest over a white shirt. Wispy white hair skimmed his shoulders, but his posture was straight. I'd peg him for late sixties. "Morning. Are you the lady I spoke to from the paper?"

I smiled and held my hand out. "Yes. Avery Winters. Pleased to meet you, Mr Curio." That was the name he'd given us. I suspected it wasn't on his birth certificate.

He shook my hand and smiled. "Welcome, welcome." He eyed the cabinet behind me. "So, what do you think of my museum so far?"

I would try and be as honest as possible. "It's… different."

"That's right. There's nothing like this anywhere in England." I was guessing that was for a very good reason.

I pulled out my notebook and pen. "What made you want to start the museum?"

"I've always found everyday objects fascinating. One man's trash is another man's treasure, as they say. What really motivated me was that my immediate circle of friends and family weren't as enamoured by dust bunnies"—he gave a nod towards the cabinet containing the royal detritus—"as I was. It was a great disappointment to me, but I reasoned that if I enjoyed these fascinations, others would, too, and it was my duty to support these people. It was a brilliant way to bring my passion into my daily life, don't you think?"

My grin was genuine. "Indeed." His idea might be a bit on the nutso side, but his motivations were noble, and his enthusiasm was infectious. "How did you get your hands on the royal dust?"

A conspiratorial grin lit his face. "A friend of mine at that time worked as a cleaner at Kensington Palace. She thought my request rather odd, but she collected it for me nonetheless."

"Out of all the animals you could have greeting visitors, why the dung beetle?"

He waggled a playful finger at me. "Ooh, you're good at this, aren't you?! Wonderfully insightful questions, young lady."

I chuckled. "Why thank you."

"The dung beetle is my spirit animal. He delves within the richness of dirt and cast-off organic matter of animals." I would've disputed his "richness" adjective, but this wasn't my story to tell.

"He lives happily in conditions others would find questionable and is therefore always in an enviable position to enjoy anything life dumps on him." A definite twinkle sparked in his eyes. And I didn't miss the dump reference. Seemed he had a sense of humour. "Why don't I show you my favourite exhibit."

"Let's go."

He hurried down the aisle, heading towards the rear of the building. For an older man, he was quick. He stopped at the very back. A large rectangular fish tank sat on a black industrial-style table.

As I reached the tank, the sharp, offensive odour of cow manure stripped my nostril hairs from their roots. The smell was potent, concentrated, and I didn't care if I offended him when I slammed my hand over my nose and mouth.

He looked at me and chuckled. "You get used to it." *Yeah, nah, I don't think so.* He leaned forward and bent, his nose almost touching the glass. "Look at my babies."

I coughed and peered closer. The quicker we did this, the quicker I could get some breathable air. Miniature versions of the car park sentry burrowed and crawled in the bottom layer of black soil and upper layer of brown manure. I gagged, held my breath, and whipped my phone out. I stepped back, my voice strangled. "Why don't I take a quick photo?"

He smiled. "Great idea!"

Macpherson paid me well, but some days it wasn't enough.

Photos taken, the first thing I spied while frantically glancing around was a skeleton standing out of smelling distance. "Ooh, would you look at that!" I hurried to it. The nameplate said George. "Hello, George. Where are you from?"

"My name's not George, wench. It's William Burgess." I jerked my gaze to the right. A man about my height stood there, arms folded, feet widespread. He looked to be in his thirties and wore pirate gear, replete with cutlass. Had he died whilst in costume for a play or party, or was he an actual pirate? At least I was assuming he was a ghost and didn't work here.

Curio reached us and stood where William was. The spirit gave him a dirty look and stepped to the side. The museum owner shivered and rubbed his arms. "This place has unusual draughts sometimes."

Okay, so it *was* a ghost. "Can you tell me about this skeleton?" There wasn't a label, except for the name.

"It dates from the seventeenth century." He approached the skeleton and put his arm around its bony shoulders.

"Get your hands off me!" The pirate swore and put his hands around Curio's neck and squeezed, but nothing happened, except Curio shivered again and stepped away from the skeleton.

"Where did you get it?" There was nothing I could do about their argument, so the best course of action was to get the interview done.

"A government auction. Apparently, George spent many years in a storeroom because no museums wanted him."

"That's not why." His gravelly voice vibrated with anger. "I was arrested for piracy, but instead of jailing me, they killed me. No trial, no nothing. They were probably trying to hide what happened." Yikes, that was sad, but then again, pirates weren't exactly known for being warm and fuzzy. And there was no going back, so even if I kind of sympathised with him, there was nothing I could do about it. Hmm. That gave me an idea for a new article.

"Did they say what George did for a living?"

"It's *not* George, you witless, dung-eating cretin!" William bellowed. I ignored the ghost, who raised his arms above his head, looked at the ceiling, and cussed up a storm.

"I have no idea. They had no information, except for the rough date of his death and that he was a relatively young man. Hence why I don't have information on a card." It was at least good to know he didn't make stuff up about the items. That dust bunny really was royal.

"Hmm, he could've been a pirate. I wonder how much money he stole and how many men he killed."

William smiled, satisfaction and pride radiating from him. "We raided a royal ship once, and I gave my beloved a token care of King Louis XV. It was the grandest emerald and diamond necklace you've ever seen." Was he bragging or telling the truth? Surely the authorities would've been searching for it, although the English may not have cared about the French king's missing jewels. In any case, I had lots of information to go on, except the name of his beloved. A scowl descended on his face. "Except the royal witch cursed me to be stuck wherever my skeleton was." That was a high price to pay for stealing royal jewels.

Curio laughed. "You have a vivid imagination, young lady. Maybe you should be writing fiction instead of articles."

"I enjoy telling people's stories. If I didn't imagine how it might be, I'd never ask the probing questions. There's often a story within a story." I observed him. What was his story within a story? "How long have you run this museum?"

His expression turned pensive. "When I was twenty-one, my father died and left me this building. It seemed like the perfect opportunity. My two siblings resented the gift, but they were ten years older than me, and had fallen out with my father. They were advised not to take it to court because they'd probably lose. In any case, they haven't spoken to me since." He looked from one side of the building to the other. "My mother died twelve years ago. This is all I have in my life."

"You never married?"

"No. It seems many women have an aversion to my passion and life's work. I've been called boring too many times to count." His sad smile poked at my heart. So, this was the story within a story. Instead of the slightly mocking tone I was going to use for the article, I'd make it humorous but not at the expense of the owner. It had just turned into a sympathetic piece that would hopefully get people to come and visit.

"Well, then, why don't we look at the rest of your life's work? I'd be honoured to find out all about what you have here."

His grateful smile warmed my insides like a sip of freshly brewed tea. Who wanted to write fiction when the truth was way more interesting? Now, to get that other information from William and I'd call it a day well used.

CHAPTER 6

Not wanting to walk home past the supermarket just in case Adam was waiting for me, I parked near the office rather than at home. This morning's interview had given me an exciting lead to follow up. I had much research to do. It was a shame I couldn't tell my colleagues about what I was doing... although, I probably could. I just wouldn't tell them the truth about how I'd come to want to write the article.

At the door to Macpherson's building, Charles appeared. "Hey, Avery."

I took my phone out of my bag and put it to my ear. "Hey, Charles. Long time no see. Where have you been?" He hadn't visited for five days. Having said that, I hadn't called him either. Work had been busy, and Meg and I visited London on Sunday and had a wander around. Meg thought it was weird to go all that way for one day, but us Aussies were used to travelling long distances for not much time, and I managed to talk her into it. I was keen to get back there because there was so much to see. The only issue was the plethora of ghosts. Being a highly populated place for a long time meant there were a ridiculous number of ghosts. Some were easy to pick on the street because they wore period clothing, but it made for crowded streets, and I didn't always know I didn't have to step around someone. Meg gave me confused side-eye glances a couple of times. I really needed to figure out how to either banish them from my sight or figure out how to peg them for ghosts as soon as I saw them.

He scrunched his face up. "Oh, has it? How long?"

"About five days."

"Oh, okay. Seems like a couple of days. Anyhoo, I wanted to warn you that there's this really pushy ghost. He died recently, and he's been asking around about you, attempting to discover where you work, and trying to get access to your apartment."

I groaned. "You wouldn't be talking about Adam by any chance, would you?" I glanced around, hoping that saying his name wouldn't conjure him.

"Yeah, that's his name. I didn't tell him anything, and I put the word out so no one talks to him."

"Thanks, buddy." Unfortunately, it was only a matter of time before he discovered I worked here, and that would be the end of my peace and quiet. "Is there any way to banish ghosts from my presence?"

His lower lip pushed out as he pondered my question. "Hmmm. I don't know. I do know someone who might be able to help. She's an alive person."

"Oh, okay. Who and where?" A combination of nerves and excitement vibrated in my belly. It would be so incredible to have someone to talk to about this who wouldn't automatically assume I was crazy. But old habits died hard. It would be challenging to admit to seeing ghosts. Yes, I'd told a couple of people—the recipients of letters from the dead—but they were in crisis at the time and believed me because what I'd had to tell them couldn't have come from anywhere else. I figured they weren't about to find me and tell everyone I knew, especially when I'd helped them.

"Celeste Portico." He gave me an address in Exeter, and I put the deets into my phone.

"Thanks. So, how're things in your world?"

He shrugged. "Same, same. Things don't change much. Do you need help with anything? I'm kinda bored."

"Haven't you been helping out at the police station?"

"Nah. It's not as much fun if I'm not helping you. Besides, I'm there for you, not me. Sergeant Fox has the ghost stuff covered. He doesn't need me." His voice wasn't super down, but I detected a hint of dejection. I knew Charles and Sergeant Fox had formed a friendship, and the sergeant had become a father figure to the younger ghost. Not that Charles was the young boy he was when he died. He'd existed for way longer than me. The way things worked still confused me. Charles was older yet not. Go figure.

"What about when they're really busy?"

"Yeah, Sergeant Fox asks me to do little things. So, do you need help with anything?"

I smiled. "Actually, I do." I told him about William the pirate. "Do you think you find out whether he knows about his descendants and who might have the jewel now? Maybe also find out more about his life and what led him to be a pirate." I had my own history book right here. Charles could get the story straight from the pirate's mouth. Not all people got to be ghosts linked to this plane, but how many were still here from maybe even a thousand years ago? What could I discover? What historical *facts* were wrong, and what could I change with a ghost's truth? I frowned, disappointment a bucket of cold reality in the face. There wouldn't be enough hours in the day to take that on. I had my hands full with just the local crimes and articles. Well, it was exciting for the four-point-five seconds I considered it.

He grinned. "Yes, totally! I'll visit him right now. See ya, Avery!"

Before I could say goodbye, he disappeared. I checked one more time for Adam, then hurried inside and up to the office.

"Aves!" Carina smiled enthusiastically and waved from her desk. Finnegan gave a nod, his expression serious.

"Hey, Carina." I grinned, then moved my gaze to Finn. "Such an understated greeting, Vinegar. Where's the fanfare, streamers, frantic waving? You should take notes from Carina."

He smiled. "Fair enough. Sorry. Just stressing about this stupid article."

"It's okay, Finny. It'll be great. Voters deserve to know d'e trut'."

"And you can back up your claims with proof?" I asked. Publishing something hard-hitting about powerful people did leave us open to being sued, but if we were writing provable truth, they didn't have a leg to stand on.

"Of course. And I know, it's just, I don't just want it to be good. I want it to be the best thing I've ever written."

I smiled. "I can relate." My smile fell. "The greatest things I ever wrote were ruined by my evil ex claiming he wrote them. He handed them in and gave me credit as a researcher/cowriter." My face heated with anger and embarrassment. All this time and I still let it get to me. Never again would I be so naïve and stupid.

Finnegan cringed, and Carina's eyes bugged out. Her face contorted in anger. "I know you've told me this stuff before, but it still makes me livid. What a stinking pillock."

I shook my head quickly, like a dog shaking off water. "Anyway, all I'm saying is, you've got this, Vinegar. If anyone can do this article justice and get the attention of the people, it's you." I smiled.

He blinked and stared at me. It was sad that he looked so surprised. Maybe I wasn't the only one whose family hadn't supported their choices? I hadn't had any in-depth conversations with him about his family. I really had no idea what his growing-up years were like. "Thanks. I'd better get back to it." His gaze fell to his computer screen. Carina shook her head slowly and pressed her lips together. We shared a "look."

"I guess I'd better get to it too."

Carina sighed. "You two are no fun. I suppose I'll get back to work, too, d'en."

A sneak attack of the warm and fuzzies spread through my chest. Even if we were all working, it was comforting having them in the same space. I hadn't known what I'd find when I came here, but this wasn't it. I figured my life would be better—because how could it have been any worse?—but I'd found people I could trust and rely on, be myself with (well, almost all of myself), just when I thought those kinds of people maybe didn't exist.

By the time I started writing my museum article, I'd forgotten all about Adam.

❦

After work, I walked to my car. Just as I reached it, Adam popped into existence, between me and my door. Not that I couldn't reach through him, but it was a surprise, and I halted and gave him a dirty look.

He had an okay face, if you didn't mind squished noses that had been broken and not fixed properly. With his average face, physique, and local-hero status, I could concede that women threw themselves at him. I was not one of them. He folded his arms. "Hey, sugar, have you calmed down yet?"

"Funnily enough, I was calm approximately twenty seconds ago. Now, not so much." And possum poo. I was talking to my car. I grabbed my phone out of my bag and spoke into it. "Get out of my way."

"Not until you agree to help find my killer."

"I'm not going to help you." I really needed to call that woman and find out how to deal with unwanted spirits. At least he couldn't hurt me. Maybe this would be good practice for keeping bad men out of my life. If only I'd had this experience before meeting Brad.

He looked me up and down, then licked his lips. "Come on, sexy. Don't be like that."

This guy was bad news, and I had the heebie-jeebies to prove it. "Ew. Get lost. Has anyone ever told you, you're a creep? Because you are. You're icky, and if you were alive, I'd kick you in the nuts." A woman walking past gave me a weird look. Oops. Even being on the phone wouldn't help with that comment. Adam scowled and called me an insult that rhymed with shut. "Wow, sucks to be you, then. If that's what I was and I'm rejecting you, that makes you doubly undesirable."

His forehead wrinkled as he considered things. He swallowed

whatever he was going to say. With a bit of luck, he was figuring out that threatening me wasn't going to work. "Look, the police are hopeless. They haven't found who did it. You might not like me, but what about my teammates? Do you want their deaths on your head?"

Surely not all his teammates could be as bad as him, but still, this wasn't my circus. "I'm sorry, but I don't have time."

"You're a cold b—"

I put my hand up. "You're not winning any friends right now." Guilt might have burrowed into my conscience just a tad. I hated myself sometimes. Ignoring someone's pleas for help, even a horrible person's, was beyond me. "Fine. If you can show me proof that your teammates are in danger from the killer, I'll help. Do you have any?"

"There should be a note in my locker at the club. I put it there after I took it from under my windscreen."

"Surely the police went through all that? And if they have the note, they'll be looking into it, and you won't need me."

He bit his lip and stared into the distance for a moment. His eyes widened. "I was there when they went through my stuff. I don't know if they found anything. I didn't hear anyone mention it." He ran a hand down his face.

"Maybe they just bagged everything and didn't look at it properly till later?" Argh, why did I sound like I cared? "In any case, I can't access anything now. Have a think about how you can prove it and get back to me." Okay, so hopefully he wouldn't find anything, and I'd never hear from him again.

He stared at me, contorting his closed mouth. Eventually, he blew out a silent, non-existent breath. "Fine. I'll be back tomorrow." His hulking form faded, and I put my phone in my bag.

On the short drive home, I pondered whether it really was my duty to help these ghosts. Had I purposely been given a gift that I was supposed to use for the greater good, or was it random, and no entity cared what I did with it?

When I parked the car, I looked up at the ceiling. "Overseer of universes and planes of existence, what do you want from me?" I sat in the silence for a few moments and watched a sparrow hop along the top of a fence.

There was a tap on my window, and I started. Heart racing, I turned. It wasn't the creator of everything—it was just Finnegan. I chuckled and got out of the car. "Thanks for the heart attack. I was just lamenting that I needed something shocking to liven up my afternoon."

He grinned, his vivid-blue eyes sparkling. "Want to go to the pub? I just realised I don't have anything to cook for dinner, and I can't be bothered shopping."

There was no reason to say no. Work was under control, and it would be good to get this Adam business out of my brain. The only thing I really wanted to do was call that medium about sending ghosts packing, but it could wait till tomorrow. "Sounds good." Okay, so Finnegan turning up wasn't a sign from the ruler of everything, but it would have to do. And, yeah, I doth protest too much. To be honest, I couldn't think of a better way to finish the day—tasty dinner with a gorgeous man who had no expectations. Definitely winning with that. If only everything was so pleasant and simple.

CHAPTER 7

T he next morning I had nothing booked in, so I gave Charles's friend a call. It was ridiculous because she obviously believed in the supernatural, but my stomach vibrated with nerves. I didn't want to go and see her, but it was time I took some control over my ability—if there was any control to be had. Maybe there wasn't a good way to prevent ghosts contacting you. If there was a way, I needed to know. Adam was annoying, but what if a truly evil ghost wouldn't leave me alone?

"Celestial Beings, can I help you?" Her accent was way posher than I was expecting, but it did have a smooth, calm tone, so that was something.

"Um, I think so. My name's Avery, and I... I was just checking if your shop was open today." How the dickens did one ask if someone could help them ward off ghosts? Even though Charles said she was his friend, did I have the right woman? "Is this Celeste?"

"Yes, it is." The smile in her voice came through loud and clear. "Charles said you'd be calling."

Argh, thank goodness. I let my breath out in a whoosh. That made things so much easier. "Oh, okay. That's great. Actually, do I need to come in, or can we have this conversation over the phone? I wanted to know how to banish ghosts."

"I think it's best if you come in. I have an appointment free at eleven. Does that time suit you?"

"Yes, it does. Thanks so much. I guess I'll see you then." Wow, I was really doing this. Past Avery would've been bemused at the very least. She might have even called herself crazy because there was no way ghosts existed. Ha ha ha, the joke was on present Avery. Although, I was happier to be alive and discover they existed, rather than figure it out after I died. That lightning strike could've gone either way.

"Goodbye, Avery. And don't worry. This is a safe space." She hung up before I could say okay. Did she mean safe as in not dangerous, or safe as in confidential? Were ghosts more dangerous than I'd experienced? Were there ghosts who could manifest enough power to physically hurt someone? I pulled out my notebook and pen and wrote down a few questions. Knowing me, I'd be a bundle of nerves and forget everything I wanted to ask.

"Hi, Avery."

I jumped in my seat at the kitchen table and jerked my head around. "Blood-sucking leeches, Charles. Do you have to do that?"

"What else am I supposed to do? It's not like I can knock on the door." He came over and stood next to me.

"Maybe you could stand on the other side of my front door and call out?" It would at least prevent the random heart-stopping appearances.

"Fine. I can do that."

I took a sip of my coffee. "So, what brings you here?"

He grinned. "I have some information on your pirate friend."

"Ooh, do tell."

"He hasn't kept up to date with his ancestors, and he doesn't know where the jewel is, but I have the names of his lover, his daughter, and her two sons, which were his grandchildren. I know when his lover died and where she lived at the time. From there, you can hopefully trace the family tree."

"Okay, that's good. Question while I think of it. How come his lover isn't a ghost with him?"

Charles scratched his arm. "How am I supposed to know? It might be that she can't find him because he's trapped at the museum. Or the more likely reason is that she went into the next life."

"That makes sense." I chuckled.

"What's so funny?"

"Well, on earth, we say the next life. But that's the next, next life. What if there's more, like next, next, next, next lives."

His eyes widened. "Please no. I'm tired just thinking about that, and I don't even need to sleep."

"What if there's reincarnation? Would you want to come back?"

His young brow furrowed. "It depends on whether I'd have nice parents or not. If I couldn't pick my parents, then no." He stared at me, then at the ground. He looked up shyly. "If there is a way for both of us to come back, maybe... maybe you could be my mum? You're really nice, and you're smart and strong. You'd make a good mum."

I put my hand on my heart. Tears burned my eyes. "You'd make a wonderful son. If we do get to come back, I'd love to be your mum." I smiled. This kid really didn't have the earthly life he deserved. Was there some entity that decided what happened to each person? If there was, I didn't like them because they did some pretty sucky things to people. Even though I knew there was life after death, I still believed it was all random. It was too sickening to think a sentient being would make children sick or give them abusive parents. *Argh, stop thinking.*

He smiled. "I suppose I should give you those details."

"Oh, yeah, right." I wrote everything down. "Thanks for that. What else have you got on for today?"

He shrugged. "I might go hang out with Sergeant Fox, see if there's anything I can help with."

I would've asked him about whether they found a threatening note in Adam's locker, but this was one case I didn't care about. If Adam got back to me, fine, but if not, it would be a good excuse to forget about it. "Okay. If you're at the station, keep your ear out for any good cases I can write about. Let me know if something pops up."

"Will do. Bye, Avery."

"See ya."

He disappeared, and Everly appeared. Talk about ghost central this morning. "Hey, Ev. How's it going?"

She folded her arms. "Meh, the usual. Actually, I'm lying. I wanted to ask about that idiot guy who's hanging around out the front. I dislike his energy. He's creeping me out, giving off aggressive and entitled vibes." She shuddered. "It reminds me of my killer, and I don't like it. Can you get rid of him, please?"

She never talked about her death, and I knew she knew who'd done it, but she didn't want to say. I'd asked her more than once. Her answer was always the same: "I don't want to talk about it." I wasn't going to ask again. "He can't hurt you, can he?"

"Kind of."

"Kind of? Can you be more specific?" From what Charles had told me, ghosts couldn't hurt each other. Although, he'd mentioned something about the different planes the ghosts inhabited, and that some ghosts were scary. What made them scary if they couldn't hurt anyone else? That didn't make sense, now that I thought about it.

"Some ghosts have the ability to suck energy from other ghosts when we're in the earthly plane. They're what you would call poltergeists. If they syphon enough of another ghost's energy, it can wipe the other ghost from existence for good. And it makes the poltergeist stronger, capable of moving things in this plane and of hurting other ghosts and the living."

It was as if invisible fingers stroked my nape. I shivered, and all my arm hairs sprang up. "Why are you only telling me this now? How common are these poltergeists? Who stops them from killing all the ghosts? Are you in danger?" Hades. I had so many questions. So many. She sat on the chair opposite me, the table cutting her off at the waist. "Do you want me to pull it out for you?"

"Do you want to pull it out for me? I'm just floating here to be honest. I figured it's easier for you to talk to me if you're not craning your neck to look up. I can float out just a bit, and you won't even have to move the chair."

"But then I won't be able to see you properly because you'll be behind the chair."

"Oh, yeah, right." She chuckled. How could she be so relaxed after she'd just told me a poltergeist could potentially unalive her for good?

I stood, went to the other side of the table, and pulled her chair out. "There we go."

She looked at me as if I were supremely amusing, and I sat back down. "I'm telling you now because there was no need to tell you before. They're not common. Most violent people end up going straight to hell—do not pass go, do not collect two hundred pounds. But some make it to the in-between. Out of them, not all want to interact anyway. That leaves a small number who are dangerous." She stared past me to the window overlooking the street. "He can't hurt me if our spirits don't touch." Everly looked back at me. "I'm just sensitive to that energy, and I don't want it around."

"Okay. Well, it just so happens that I'm going to see a woman about it this morning. I want to be able to banish ghosts I don't want around. He's one of them." Again, I wondered how he'd managed to get so many women to fall for him. Some people did not have good radars.

Her brows drew down. "You're not going to banish me, are you?"

I looked at her as if she'd gone mad. "Um, no. Of course not. Why would I do that? This is your place, after all. You'll still be here after I'm long gone."

"You're not leaving, are you?"

"No. Not unless Mrs Crabby kicks me out. I'm happy here, but it's unrealistic to think I'll be here for years and years. It's not like I own the place. And I'm here on a working visa. If I ever lose my job, I'll have to find another one, and it might be somewhere else, or I might not get one and have to go back to Australia. Or, who knows, I might die?"

Way to catastrophise, Avery.

To be fair to myself, I'd almost died once before I came here, and I'd been targeted a couple of times by killers since I'd arrived. I seemed to find myself in these situations. Okay, so I actively sought out dangerous people. But it wasn't as if I had a death wish. Justice was important. That was all.

"You're not going to die, Miss Drama Queen."

"Are you psychic now?"

"No, but you're young and wily." She smirked. "Besides, you can't die till you and Finn get together."

"What?" I snapped my spine straighter. Why were people always trying to get me to couple up with someone? Was being single really that bad? I was rather enjoying it.

"I saw you come home last night. You guys were on a date. Nice work. He's hot."

"Oh, that. It wasn't a date. It was two friends going out for dinner. There was zero romance. Meg even joined us for five minutes." Probably because she was sussing out the situation, but still.

"Well, that's disappointing. You're boring."

My mouth fell open. "What?! I find myself fabulous company. Just because you don't appreciate my awesomeness, doesn't mean I'm not."

She laughed. "I was just joshing. Anyway, as fun as riling you up is, I have to go." She stood. "Just keep an eye out for that ghost, and if you can manage it, please move him on."

"I will for sure. See ya."

Everly disappeared. So, Adam posed a wider problem than I thought. What if there was no way to banish him? Best not consider that right now. *Worry about that if you need to later.*

Instead of stressing about everything, I called Carina and asked about whether the office had access to any ancestry websites. Turned out we did. That's where I'd start with my information on William's ancestors. I also had an address on the coast of where his lover and daughter had lived way back when. I'd check current property records and see if the names matched his grandchildren's surname. If not, I'd have a lot more digging to do. I also needed to research his pirate days, see if I could get any information on that. If I was going to tell his story, I needed facts that could be corroborated, or I'd look like an idiot. If someone accused me of making stuff up, I wouldn't be able to prove anything. And that was not a good look for a journalist.

I got to work. It didn't take long to discover that the house wasn't in the family any more. There'd been numerous transfers over the years, and when I googled it, there were two different for-sale real-estate ads for different years. So, that avenue was out.

I searched for any mention of those jewels and found none. Had they really been the French royal family's? I'd had a quick chat to William when Curio was distracted by a visitor. The pirate had mentioned the jewels were a gift from the king to a lover, and he said they was supposedly cursed, which sounded a bit far-fetched.

As it was, I didn't even have a picture of the jewels, just a basic description. Yikes. This was becoming more complicated by the second. I might have to sit down with the ghost and draw it with his guidance. Would he even remember what it looked like after so many years? And how was I going to get that kind of time with him without Curio wondering what I was doing? Because William was trapped there, it wasn't like I could visit him somewhere more private.

I checked my phone. *Argh, where did the morning go?* It was time to leave for Exeter. I jumped up, slid my computer into my bag, and grabbed my keys, tremors of both excitement and fear fluttering through me. After holding my secret in for so long, blurting it out to someone else felt dangerous, but if she could see Charles, I really had nothing to worry about.

The more pressing question I had to ask as I ran the gauntlet outside as Adam jogged after me shouting, "Hey, stop, gorgeous. I need to talk to you," was: Could she help me? I jumped in my car and slammed the door.

Right now, I needed all the help I could get.

CHAPTER 8

C elestial Beings was situated on a busy road near Exeter College on the ground floor of a three-storey brown-brick building. Candles, a pack of tarot cards, crystals, and a white coffee mug proclaiming "I heart ghosts" sat on a small, round antique table in the window. As was typical of spiritual-type shops, the cloying aroma of incense clung to me as soon as I entered. How did they not all have burned nostril hairs? That stuff was potent.

Crystals strung on silver chains hung from the ceiling, the overhead lighting sending prisms of colour randomly around the space. It was quite magical. A sense of peace cascaded over me. Two of the browsing customers turned to look at me and smiled. I returned it, then made my way past numerous tables and shelves of all kinds of knickknacks—small, colourful dragons, crystal balls, books on spirituality and witchcraft, goblets. I found the counter towards the back of the shop. A sign behind it said, Tarot readings twenty pounds.

The woman serving at the counter was about my height but looked maybe in her fifties. Her straight black hair fell to her behind. She wore a flowy sky-blue blouse over a long, white skirt, which was at odds with the plethora of tattoos on her arms and neck. She was a goth woman in a girly-girl getup. She grinned. "Ah, you must be Avery."

"Yes. Great guess."

Her grin took on a cheeky edge, and she glanced over at the customers who'd smiled at me. "They're ghosts. As soon as you smiled back, I knew. What we can do is rare. When Charles told me about you, I couldn't believe it."

Argh, I knew the first question I was going to ask her—how could I tell ghosts from real people? "I wasn't sure what to expect, coming here, to be honest. I don't make a habit of telling people about my... ability. It's fairly recent, and it's caused a lot of problems with my family." I didn't need to get into it all with her, but if I gave her some background, she'd at least know where I was coming from. "So I'd appreciate it if you didn't tell anyone." Not that she'd know anyone I knew, but with six degrees of separation, maybe something would get back to the good people of Manesbury, and I'd have to try and explain myself. That was the last thing I needed whilst finding my feet.

"Just give me a minute to shut the shop, and we can chat." The thousands of bangles on her wrists tinkled as she moved through the store.

So, there were no live people in here, except for us. Hopefully she got normal customers, too, because I was pretty sure ghosts didn't have cash or cards.

She came back, and instead of heading to the other side of the counter, she moved to the righthand side of the shop at the back. The two ghosts waved to her, and she waved back. Then she pushed the pale-aqua wall, and a door opened. Nifty. A secret room. All good tarot-card readers should have a secret room. It added to the mystique.

The square space had a round table in the middle with three seats around it. A kitchenette sat in one corner because even spooky people needed sustenance every now and again. The walls were painted a soft bronze, the ceiling black, silver stars dotting its surface. She stood behind one of the chairs and gestured. "Please, sit down. Would you like a tea or coffee?"

I pulled out a chair and sat. "I'm good, thanks. I hope you don't mind, but I have so many questions."

She turned and flicked the kettle on. "That makes two of us. As I said before—I don't often get to talk to others who are like me. I'd love to hear your experiences."

As she readied her cup of tea, I gave her the background of how I came to see ghosts and got her up to speed with what had happened since I'd arrived in the UK. When I finished, the smothering load I'd carried since this whole spirit thing started lifted off me. I blinked, surprised. Well, what did you know? Talking to someone who understood was exceedingly cathartic.

She sat and took a sip of tea. "Wow, you were really thrown into it. I discovered I could see ghosts when I was twelve. I was in a car accident and died on scene. They revived me and rushed me to hospital where I died again. Thankfully, and obviously"—she grinned—"they succeeded in bringing me back a second time." She leaned forward. "Don't worry; I'm not a ghost."

I snickered. "That was going to be one of my questions, actually. How can you tell whether someone's a ghost or alive? I can't pick to save myself, and it's getting me into awkward situations."

"One way is the temperature change when you're near them, but you have to be close, and it wouldn't work so well outside in winter." She cradled her tea. "One thing I've found that works is obsidian." She reached into her top, lifted out a necklace, and let the teardrop obsidian stone rest just under her clavicle. "When this sits next to your skin, ghosts take on a faded appearance. They don't become see-through—it's more like there's a faint rose-coloured film between us and them."

"Really?" I didn't want to sound sceptical, but it was just a rock. I'd always thought the crystal healing stuff was a load of poppycock. But Charles trusted her, and she could see ghosts, so I'd at least try it. I might feel stupid doing it, but if it worked, I could stop worrying I was being weird.

She smirked. "Yes, really." She took her necklace off and handed it to me. "Here. Try it. Hold it and go into the shop. Beatrice and Larry will still be out there. This is their haunt."

I took the necklace and closed my fingers over the stone, nestling the obsidian in my palm. It was warm from being under Celeste's shirt, which was minorly icky, like sitting on a toilet still heated from someone else's behind.

I went back into the shop and found the ghosts giggling at the door as they watched a squirrel run after someone who was walking while eating. The ghosts were, indeed, covered by a rosy haze. They turned and gave me quizzical looks.

"Oh, sorry, just trying out an obsidian stone."

"Ah." The woman smiled. "It's grand to find someone else who can see us." She turned to her male companion. "Isn't it, love?"

He nodded. "It is. Being invisible loses its appeal after a while."

"Do you ever hang out with other ghosts?"

The lady rolled her eyes. "He says he doesn't want to because they're dead."

Was that like being prejudiced? So strange. "Oh, okay. Anyway, I'll just be getting back to Celeste now." I turned and made my way back to her lunchroom.

"Did it work?" she asked as I sat.

"Yep. Thank you." I handed it back to her. "Do you have any for sale? I'll gladly buy one."

"No you won't. I'll give you one. It's a welcome-to-the-seeing-dead-people-group present." Her eyes wrinkled at the corners as she smiled.

"Are you sure?" I hated getting free stuff. I always felt like I was ripping off the other person.

"Positive. Do you have any other questions?"

"Definitely. How do I get rid of annoying or dangerous ghosts?"

Her expression shifted, and the light-hearted mood disappeared. "You can't, at least not permanently." She slowly spun her teacup around and around on its saucer. Eventually, her gaze met mine. "Are you having a problem?"

"Sort of. I mean, I don't feel like I'm in danger, but there's a ghost who won't leave me alone. He wants me to solve his murder and won't take no for an answer. He's not a very nice soul." I couldn't exactly call him a person because he wasn't one any more.

"It made me realise that some ghosts might be even worse, and I don't want to have to deal with it. Another ghost mentioned that poltergeists existed, and that they can physically hurt people or ghosts." I shivered. Just thinking about it gave me the creeps. What I would do to go back to the time before I knew spirits existed. Hmm, that was only partly true. I didn't want to go back to living with Brad or being beholden to my parents. I sighed. Knowing about ghosts was actually a small price to pay for being free of my negative past.

"That ghost was right, unfortunately. Like any other ghost, poltergeists can't come into your home without an invitation, but they can be in what used to be their own place, or they can go to a place of business. There is a way to banish ghosts for a short while, but it only lasts a day or two at most, and depending on how powerful a poltergeist is, you won't be able to banish one. You'll need a priest or witch for that."

Priest or *witch*? Also, that sucked big time. "Do you mean a witch like in movies, or a witch who celebrates Beltane and the winter solstice?"

She laughed. "The Beltane/solstice type. I didn't know there were any others. Earth magic exists, but the stuff you see on TV isn't real." I didn't fancy having to call a priest to my house. Images of the movie *Poltergeist* came to mind.

Giving up on the idea of protecting myself from evil spirits, I moved on. "So, how do I banish annoying ghosts?"

"You'll need a blue zircon, which I'll get for you before you leave."

Everything shouldn't come down to money, but in my world, it often did. "How much are they?"

She gave me a look as if to say "don't be silly." "I'll give it to you."

"No! I won't accept two gifts. If you don't let me pay, I'll leave without it and get it somewhere else." Was that too mean? I just didn't deserve it was all. "I only asked because I have no idea if they're ten pounds or five hundred." Okay, so if they were five hundred, it would be unlikely she'd offer it for free.

"I sell them for anywhere between fifteen pounds and three hundred. I only stock ones that jewellers don't want. Some stones go for thousands."

"Oh, wow."

"The crystal I'll give you... sell you, will be a rough, barely polished one. It'll just look like a pretty stone."

"As long as it does the job, I don't care what it looks like." Well, I wouldn't want it to look like a lump of poo, but if it helped me, I wasn't going to be picky.

"Good. You hold the crystal in your palm and say, "Spirit from another plane, return in haste to whence you came. Also imagine you're shutting the door on them. It helps to focus your energy." She said this as if it were the most normal thing in the world. What energy was she talking about? Brain electricity, my metabolism, or was I supposed to be channelling something from somewhere else? This seemed rather vague. But she'd been kind so far, so all I could do was try. I had nothing to lose... unless someone saw me doing it.

"Can I say that in my head, or does it have to be out loud?"

"Out loud, of course."

Of course.

"And cleanse them every month by leaving them in the light of the full moon for the night."

"Cleanse them?" I really had no idea about all this woo-woo crystal stuff.

"Yes. They gather negative energy when you use them and when they're sitting around, especially if they're in stressful environments." She touched her chest over where I assumed the onyx sat.

"Okay, I'll make sure to cleanse them." I resisted the urge to shake my head. So many things I'd thought were full of baloney were turning out to be real. Was there somewhere I could draw the line? At this rate, the next thing I'd be doing was getting my aura read and sprinkling salt on my windowsills.

My phone rang. I gave Celeste an apologetic look and took it out of my bag. My eyes widened at the name on the screen. What did Bellamy want? "Hello, Sergeant Bellamy. How's it going?"

"Hello, Ms Winters. I was wondering if I could have a chat to you down at the station." He didn't sound angry, so at least I wasn't in trouble… for now.

"Ah, yes. What's it about?"

"I'd rather not say over the phone. Can you come down today? It's rather urgent." If I didn't know better, it sounded as if he were stressed, but it wasn't with me. What was going on?

"Of course. I could be there in half an hour or so."

"Good-oh. I'll see you then." He hung up. I looked at Celeste. "I'm so sorry. That was the police sergeant in my local area. We haven't always been on great terms, so I don't want to annoy him by keeping him waiting."

Her serene expression told me she wasn't offended. "That's fine. I'm just glad I could meet you."

"Do you have any important advice before I go? Maybe we could catch up again and chat. I have other questions. Plus, it's so nice to be able to talk about this stuff without people thinking I'm crazy."

She stood. "I hear you. As for advice, just don't promise ghosts help if you don't have time because they will, literally, haunt you until you've delivered. As for poltergeists—they're rare, but if you come across one who has it in for you, stand up to them. Don't let them scare you. Let me know if you have problems, and I'll put you onto a priest I've dealt with in the past."

I stood and grabbed my bag. "Okay, sounds good. Thanks for everything. You've been so helpful, and I really appreciate it. Next time, why don't I interview you for the paper?"

"That would be excellent, thank you." She came around the table and gave me a hug. "Don't be a stranger."

I smiled. "I won't."

We went out to the counter, and she gave me two stones—one black, and one the colour of a clear sky… not unlike Finnegan's eyes, or maybe a shade lighter. I internally rolled my eyes at my comparison. I was such a teenager sometimes.

Thankfully, Celeste let me pay for the zircon, which was rather pretty, even though it was the fifteen pound one. It was an irregular shape, bumpy but with a smooth surface, and the size of a Matchbox car.

"It's easier if you put them on a chain. I always lose things that small." She laughed.

"I'll look into that." For now, I'd just have to have them in my handbag. Maybe I could hold the onyx when I walked around outside. "Thanks again. You've been really kind."

"It's been my pleasure." She wandered to the front door and unlocked it. "Hopefully I'll see you soon. Text me your number."

"Okay, will do."

"Good luck, Avery."

"Thanks. I'm going to need it."

CHAPTER 9

"Come in," Bellamy called from inside his office. I entered, and he stood and gestured to one of the chairs on the other side of his desk. "Thanks for coming, Ms Winters. Please take a seat." Sergeant Fox wasn't here, and neither was Charles. Were they checking out something interesting?

I sat and placed my hands in my lap. He didn't seem angry with me, and I was pretty sure I hadn't done anything to annoy him lately, so I relaxed. "I won't lie—I'm curious as to why I'm here." I wasn't into suspense. The sooner he revealed what he wanted, the better.

He sat. "It's about the Murphy case." He picked up his stapler, glanced at it, and placed it back on the table. Whatever he was about to say, he didn't want to. Interesting. Was he about to ask for help? Stranger things had happened. Lots of stranger things in fact. "We've been gathering evidence." His hand strayed to the stapler again and rested on it. "The case is moving along at the usual pace, but we don't have any firm suspects yet." He stared at the stapler. For goodness' sake. This was going to take all day.

"But? Isn't that the way it usually works?"

He met my gaze. "When it's a crime of opportunity, it's harder to unravel." He pressed his lips together. "It also works that way when the mayor of Exeter isn't the uncle of the deceased victim." And there we went.

There was no trophy—a rugby trophy no less—at the scene of the crime. I was the only one who knew about it... oh, and the killer. The subject matter had led me to surmise it was either someone associated with his rugby or someone who hated rugby. Which meant it wasn't random, but, again, I couldn't tell Bellamy that. "How do you think I can help? And, with all due respect, who cares if he's the mayor's nephew? He's just another person. What about all the other people who need crimes solved? He needs to get in line." Okay, so you would think I'd jump at the chance, but I wanted to know what his expectations were before I agreed. Maybe I'd lost my marbles. Hadn't I been waiting weeks and weeks for Bellamy to take me seriously and give me inside info? Now I was questioning it. Maybe it was also because I didn't like the victim.

Bellamy cleared his throat. "Ordinarily, you would think so, but this is politics, and while the mayor doesn't have a lot of clout over police matters, one of his best mates is the Minister for Crime and Policing. He kindly reminded me of that fact when he called. I could find myself looking at a demotion or early retirement if I don't come up with the goods. We might solve it quickly, but it might drag on for months. The evidence is at forensics, and the body's with the coroner, but we haven't even got a motive. Everyone at the club loved him, the women loved him, the fans loved him. All we can figure is that it was a crime of opportunity. The only issue with that is nothing was stolen from the supermarket, and he still had his wallet in his back pocket."

Could I try and steer him in the rugby direction, or at least in the direction of "it wasn't random?" "Maybe the murderer got spooked? The other angle could be that it was actually someone who knew him. Wouldn't jealousy be a good motive? Maybe he peed off the wrong woman? Maybe one of his teammates was jealous of his popularity? Does he have siblings who aren't equally appreciated?"

He cocked his head to the side, irritation in the press of his closed lips. "Of course we're looking at those angles, but nobody's talking, and we have no leads in that direction. We have a lot more people to interview. Why couldn't he have been a tennis player—do you know how many teammates he has?" He leaned his head on the chairback and blew out a loud breath.

Bellamy, as much as he'd pushed back against me having access to more police information, was a good guy. He cared about his community, and he was Finnegan's family friend. Besides, I was making some headway—he trusted me more now than he did when I first arrived, and he'd acknowledged I'd solved crimes before they had. "How do you think I can help though. It's not like I'm psychic." Okay, I could see ghosts, but I wasn't going to tell him that. Let him think all my information was because of my own smarts.

"People like talking to you—they let their guard down. When we turn up, people are automatically on the defensive. You have a knack for getting to the bottom of things, too, which is what's required of a good journalist. I want to harness those skills. I'm happy to pay you consultancy fees, and if you're worried about your job with MacPherson, don't. I called him and asked before I called you. He wants the scoop on the article when we arrest someone, and I said I'd be happy for you to break the story."

I blinked. Wow, he was super serious. The mayor must be a jerk and a half. I hated people who pushed others around. I disliked the victim, but my desire to help Bellamy was way stronger. Looked like I'd have to suck up my misgivings and do the right thing. "Okay, I'll help."

He smiled and relaxed into his chair. "Thank you, Ms Winters. Aren't you going to ask how much consultancy fees are?"

"Oh, yeah. How much are they?" I should've been excited about the extra money, but funnily enough, it hadn't been why I'd said yes.

"Ninety pounds an hour. Depending on the skill we're asking for, it can be much higher, but in this case, that's what it is. I hope that's okay. You'll be responsible for your own taxes and any expenses you incur in the course of the investigation, like petrol and phone calls. Keep track of your hours and submit an invoice to me on the Friday of each week. The department pays sixty days after receiving the invoice." Hmm, that was a long time, but I wasn't doing this solely for the money, and what else should I expect from a government department? At least it was fantastic money. I'd never made that much.

I laughed. "I think I can make do." I also got an article out of it at the end, and a chance for the bonus since this was a big case. It would probably be shared with MacPherson Media's other outlets too. "Would you like me to start today? And do you have any information you'd like to give me now or instructions?"

He shook his head. "Not at the moment. I'd like to see what you come up with without any influence. Choose your own angle and go for it. When you've had a chance to interview a few people, let me know, and we'll have a meeting, say, in two days? Speak to as many people as you can. I'll email you the details of his friends and family. Oh, and I also need you to sign an NDA. You're not to discuss this with anyone outside of this office—not Finn, not the victim's parents, not Meg, not the mayor—even if he threatens you—no one." He reached to his right and pulled a file across the desk, took out a document, and slid it over to me. "It's standard, but take five minutes to read it now. When it's signed, I'll have it copied, and you can take the copy with you."

If the mayor threatened me, he'd get an earful. I was done with people bullying me, and if he wanted to escalate things, I'd write a lovely piece on him and kill his career. I picked up the NDA and read all three pages. It said I could only speak about it when a suspect was arrested, but even then, certain facts would have to be withheld from my article so the case could go to court in a way that was fair and wouldn't damage the prosecution's case. Bellamy would get the final say on my article. That all seemed fair. I scrawled my signature and slid it back. "Done."

His serious expression was cast asunder by a smile. He stood and reached across the table. "Welcome to the team."

I stood and smiled. Today had been the weirdest day in a while, and that was saying something. I shook his hand. "Happy to be aboard. Let's get this mayor off your back."

"Yes, let's."

And that was how I finally shimmied my way into the Cranston-bury police and insider information. Now I just needed to earn my keep and solve the crime, or this could be the last time I was allowed to set foot in the station. No pressure. No pressure at all.

CHAPTER 10

There was only one problem with being a journalist and not a police officer—people could refuse to talk to you. When I called Adam's coach, Toby Atherton—the young, cranky man—he said he didn't want to speak to me. He also demanded to know where I got his number because it wasn't readily available, and the club didn't give that information to just anyone. I told him I was a journalist and had my ways. He hung up.

The next person I considered calling was the creepy assistant coach, but I wasn't ready to go there yet. If I could get information out of someone else at the club, I might not have to talk to him at all.

They had training again this evening, and I made my way there after an early dinner. I wore casual clothes so I didn't look so official. Rather than announce my presence, I skulked around the clubhouse, which was unlocked. If I could pick people off and chat to them without the coach knowing, I'd have longer with them. The last thing I needed was for him to order everyone not to talk to me.

The entry room had brown tile floors, a staircase to a higher level, and three doors off it. A door to the left said Women's Change

Rooms, and the door to the right said Men's Change Rooms. I stopped to listen. Nope, it was unlikely that anyone was in either of them. I headed for the third door, which was directly opposite the entry and looked to connect with a hallway.

The dark corridor led left and right, faint illumination coming from a flickering single fluorescent light on the ceiling. Talk about dingy. I picked left and tiptoed past a couple of closed doors. As I neared the end of the passageway, someone sniffled loudly. I froze, my heart hammering. I turned, ready with an excuse as to why I was creeping around the building, but there was no one there. It must've come from the last door on the right. A narrow line of light spilled from the barely open door. I crept closer, my ears primed. I stopped as near to the door as I dared and glanced behind me. Coast was clear that way.

The sniffling morphed into crying. A woman's voice said, "Cath, it's going to be okay. I promise."

"But he was cheating on me with Melissa. I look like such an idiot. I hate him." Someone—I'm assuming the upset one—blew their nose.

"When did you find out?"

A pause. More nose blowing. "You have to promise not to tell anyone." Another pause. "Promise, or I won't say. And if you do tell anyone, I'll lie about it." Yikes. They had to be talking about Adam, didn't they?

A chill seeped over me, goosebumps sprouting along my arms.

"Hey, sexy. What are you doing, sneaking around here?" Argh, it was Adam. I wasn't going to engage, though, because the women in there would hear me, and we were about to get to the good bit. "Stop ignoring me. I know you can hear me."

I turned and glared and slammed my pointed finger over my closed lips in the universal sign for shut up; then I pointed at the door. If only Bellamy's job wasn't on the line.

"Okay, Cath. I promise. I won't say anything to anyone."

"I found out a week before he was killed. I wanted to say something, but I didn't want to lose him. He would've left her if I'd told him to, at least I think so, but I didn't know, and I needed to think everything through. Now everyone's found out he was cheating on me because of that big mouth whore playing the grieving girlfriend."

"That's awful. I'm sorry. But he didn't love her. He loved you. She was just a fling. Practically every guy on the team's had her. Except Henry, of course." Henry must be her boyfriend or something. Hopefully, she was right.

Adam huffed. "Cath's a drama queen. She'll get over it. Besides, I didn't love either of them. They were convenient. Why do women always make things into something they aren't? I never told her I loved her."

I turned to look at him. His "whatever" expression made me want to outer axe him in the throat. Shame he was a ghost.

Cath started crying again. This was my cue, and Cath was now suspect number one. I crept back down the hall a short way, then walked with purpose, making noise so they could hear me coming. They'd never guess I'd been listening. I stopped at the partly open door and knocked.

Someone sucked in a breath. Not-Cath said, "Come in."

I pushed the door open to a small office and gave a polite smile, as if I didn't know that a drama had been playing out but was still mindful that someone close to the club had recently died. "Hi, I'm Avery Winters. I'm doing a story on Adam for the *Manesbury Daily*, and I was wondering if I could have a quick chat to you ladies. I'm trying to build a profile on the sort of person he was. So far everyone's had lovely things to say about him."

Cue two women staring at me. Cath was easy to pick—she was the one sitting down. A brunette with bloodshot, red-rimmed eyes and gripping a tissue. Not-Cath stood next to her. A tall redhead in business attire who looked slightly older than her friend. I'd peg them both for early twenties.

Not-Cath rearranged her expression to a polite, businesslike one. "I'm sorry, but we have nothing to say at this time. We're in a meeting."

"Oh, no problem. I'm going to speak to his girlfriend next." I took my notepad out of my bag and looked at a random page, then straight at Cath. "Melissa, I believe her name is."

Cath's lips pinched together, and fire blazed in her eyes. Gotcha. "Don't put that slag's name in the paper! She wasn't his girlfriend; I was. We were living together." She jumped to her feet, tears in her eyes. "I couldn't stand it if you gave her airtime. Please don't. I'll tell you everything you want to know if you promise not to interview her. I'll even send you a picture of the two of us you can use in the paper." Not-Cath was looking at her as if she'd lost the plot. She probably couldn't see what all the fuss was about Adam. You and me both, not-Cath. You and me both.

Or, was she worried that Cath would incriminate herself?

"That would be lovely. Wow, I can't believe she'd lie to everyone about something like that. She must be so jealous of you." It didn't hurt to butter her up. I looked at not-Cath. "Do you both work here?"

Not-Cath folded her arms. "Yes. I manage the day-to-day running of the club, and Cath is Coach Atherton's assistant. As well as the men's teams, we manage the women's, and children's. We run the local club championship, organise buses for the away games for the guys in the bigger championships, liaise with solicitors for player contracts. All sorts of things."

"And your name is…?"

"Peta. Peta Dale."

I wrote it all down. "So, Adam was contracted to play at the club because he was a big-name player, wasn't he?"

Peta looked at me, and I didn't like the shrewdness in her eyes. Was there stuff she was going to clam up about? "Yes, he was, but the details are confidential."

"Oh, not a problem." I gave her smile. "I chatted to one of his mates who said he was the highest-paid player though. Was that right?" Liar, liar, pants on fire.

She rolled her eyes. "Yes. Honestly, I don't know why I have to sign an NDA but no one else can keep their mouths shut. I suppose it doesn't matter now that he's dead." Cath burst into tears again.

Not-Cath placed an arm around her shoulders. "I'm so, so sorry. I didn't mean to blurt it out like that."

Hang on a minute. I hadn't noticed before, because I'd assumed it was from crying, but the swelling around one of Cath's eyes was larger than the other. Bruising peeked through from the make-up that had come off from her crying and wiping with a tissue. Had she sustained a black eye attacking Adam? I feigned being impressed. "Do you ladies play in the women's division? You're so brave." I checked her hands and forearms for scratches or bruises. There were none.

Peta stared at me. She was probably trying to figure out why I'd asked that question. She wasn't stupid. Cath, on the other hand, shook her head. "No, of course not. It's way too violent. I leave it to the boys." She sighed. "Adam was so good on the field."

"Oh, okay. Do you mind if I ask how you got that shiner on your left eye? I bet it's really sore."

Peta frowned and stared at Cath's eye. "You do too. What happened?"

Cath looked from her friend to me and back again. "I was so upset the other night, crying, and I walked into the doorframe. Honestly, I did. I know it's sounds stupid, but I haven't been myself."

Peta raised her eyes and glared at me. "None of that is to make it into your paper. Am I understood?"

"Of course. This is off the record. I was just curious."

"I think this interview is over. Cath's had a rough couple of days, and I have work to do." She walked to the door and held it wider. The look on her face said she wasn't mucking around.

Not wanting to cause trouble—the last thing I needed was Peta banning me from the club—I gave a nod. "Of course. I'm so sorry you're all suffering. I hope things get better for you, Cath."

She looked at me, a forlorn expression on her face. "Thanks. I hope so too."

When I left, I headed straight to my car, but Adam was cold on my heels. "So, have you decided to help me?"

I kept walking. "No." It was true. I wasn't doing this to help him.

A sharp chill seized my upper arm as Adam tried to grip it.

"Stop walking when I'm talking to you. Keep pushing me and you'll regret it."

I started jogging, leaving him behind, and the burning cold stopped. As I reached my car, I delved into a small pocket inside my bag and grabbed the protection stone. What in Hades was I supposed to say again? Why hadn't I practiced this?

Adam stood in front of me, face a thundercloud, his icy eyes full of rage. The irises were almost all black. My heart raced, and my palms sweated. Thank the gods he couldn't lay a hand on me. My amygdala didn't know that though, and my feet wanted to take me far away. But I stood my ground, and finally the words came to me. I imagined a door between planes and me shoving him through. All my anger and fear pushed out my whispered, "Spirit from another plane, return in haste to whence you came."

His eyes widened, and his mouth opened to say something, but I didn't hear it because his form distorted and swirled as if he was water being sucked through a drain. Then he disappeared.

I leaned against my car, bent and put my hands on my thighs, and drew heaving breaths. *Oh my God it worked. It really worked.* Relief and amazement curled my lips into a smile. *It's okay now, Avery. He's just a ghost. He can't hurt you.* How long did I have? Twenty-four hours? It wasn't enough, but I'd be ready next time.

I straightened and gazed around. No one had seen me freaking out. Thank Hades. My legs were jelly, but my hand wasn't shaking, and I managed to unlock the car with no dramas, but I did fall into my seat. Damn spirits. I swung my legs inside and shut the door. That was a situation I didn't want to repeat. I shut my eyes and took slow, deep breaths. There were still people to talk to tonight. Once my heart rate had returned to normal, I opened my eyes and considered what I needed to do next.

I'd wait till training was over and nab one of the players when he was at his car. I could pick my moment—one where none of the coaches or Peta were around. I also called Macpherson.

"Winters, it's after hours. Is everything all right?"

Incoming lie. "I'm fine, thanks. I just have a favour to ask. I've just interviewed Adam's live-in girlfriend, and she's really upset. I thought it might be nice for the paper to send her some flowers. She works at the club, too, so it might make them more amenable to talking to me further, you know, so we can help Bellamy."

Hesitation was never a good sign. I waited though. He'd eventually answer. "Why do we *need* to send flowers?"

"Are you insinuating I did something to upset someone?"

"It wouldn't be the first time one of my journalists put their foot in it." His tone was light, so at least I wasn't in mega trouble.

"I didn't upset anyone... exactly. The person in question was already crying when I approached her. She and the manager of the club were talking. I spoke to them, but the impression I got was that the manager didn't want the other woman—Adam's girlfriend— telling me too much. I feel like it would be to our benefit if we sent her flowers. She is a grieving girlfriend, after all. We need to send it via the club though—I want the manager on our side too. It's going to take a bit of work. They were clamming up on me."

"Hmm, you make fair points. Consider it done, Winters. So, how's it going? Bellamy is putting a considerable bit of faith in you. I don't need to tell you not to let the team down. A lot's riding on this." Wow, thanks for putting on the pressure.

"I promise I'll make you proud." My eyes widened. That popped out automatically. Talk about laying it on thick. And it wasn't like he was my father. Although, it was impossible to make him proud. The last time I'd said that to my male parental unit was when I was eight. I won the hundred metres final at the athletics carnival too. But he wasn't there to see it, and when I showed him my ribbon, he grunted and handed it back. So... it wasn't something I ever said to anybody.

"You already have, Winters. Your work has been exemplary since you've gotten here. I have no doubt you'll do well with this too. Good luck. Now, my wife is waiting for me to have dinner, so I'm over and out." The phone went dead. That was the closest to a goodbye I was ever going to get from him. Oh well.

I scrolled the internet and read the other news articles about Adam's death. There were only four, and one of them was my brief one the day of discovery. I guessed a small-time rugby player's murder wasn't that interesting to people in London. Those articles were as scant in information as I expected, although two of them mentioned the grieving uncle and had quotes from the man. Maybe it was time to make an appointment with him. He wasn't the sort of guy you could just rock up and see. Mayors were busy people. And how valuable would speaking to him be? Great for soundbites for an article, but not great for impartial information. He'd only paint the picture of his nephew he wanted me to see. Maybe I'd give it a miss.

I'd parked where I could see the action on the field. The players were coming off and crowding around the head coach. Looked like I didn't have long to wait to nab someone. Hopefully the assistant coach would leave soon, as would Peta and Cath.

Speak of the devils, the two women came around the corner of the clubhouse. I slid down until I was eye to eye with the middle of my steering wheel, my knees jammed uncomfortably against the underside of the dashboard. They turned left instead of right and didn't walk past me, nor had they seen me. Phew.

I was so silly for not thinking of it before, but I should disguise myself, or at least hide my face and hair. It was fairly late in the day, but it was still light out, and I could get away with my big sunglasses. I took them out of my bag and slid them on. Then I grabbed a plain navy-blue cap from my backseat and jammed it on. That should keep the assistant coach from recognising me at least—two creepy male confrontations in one day wasn't what I was after. I resumed a normal sitting position and waited.

It took about twenty minutes for the first players to amble into the parking area. They were chatting, a couple of them laughing, but generally the mood was sombre. The head coach was on the phone, his face pinched. When he spoke, he gesticulated wildly with his free hand. Who was he arguing with? I stayed put and crossed my fingers that he would get in his car and leave before the last of the stragglers emerged from the club.

My wish was granted—the head coach drove away, and two of his players wandered into the car park, duffel bags slung over their shoulders. Hmm, coming here meant being all cloak and dagger. I could just get a list of players from Bellamy and go see them at home. Argh, why didn't I think of that before? It would take some getting used to actually being privy to information for a change. I chuckled—Finnegan would be so jelly if he knew. Charles would probably be happy to stake this place out for me. It was a public place, so he'd be able to get inside. Hopefully I wouldn't always be this slow in life.

I took my glasses off and got out of the car, pen and notebook in hand. The young men looked about my age, one a similar height and build to Adam with a dark, short beard, the other clean-shaven, about six foot and whilst muscly was still relatively lean. Their wet hair and clean street clothes made it obvious they'd just showered. They peered at me and stopped walking. When I smiled, they smiled back. That was a good start. "Hi, I'm Avery. I'm writing a story on what Adam meant to everyone at the club, and I was wondering if you had a minute."

Their smiles fell, and they gave each other a "look." Had the coach warned everyone off speaking about it?

The bigger guy looked at me. "I don't really have anything to say. He was a good player, and the team will miss him." Hmm, what was going on?

"Oh, did the coach tell you not to talk to me?"

His forehead wrinkled. "I guess so." That looked like a cop out. I'd bet my favourite pen that the coach hadn't actually said anything, and these guys just didn't want to talk about it.

The other guy shifted from foot to foot. "I gotta go. Nice to meet you, Avery. Good luck with your article."

The bigger guy watched his friend leave, then turned to me. "Just so you know, and I don't want this quoted, not everyone loved Adam, but we like our places on the team, so we keep quiet. If you want to speak to someone who'll rave about him, talk to Joel Folkes. He'll probably be at our next training on Saturday afternoon at two."

"Okay. Thanks. Have a good evening." As he walked off, I wrote down everything that had just happened and took a sneaky pic of the guy from behind. I'd have to chase up who those two were online. Their pictures should be somewhere. So, why didn't they like

Adam, and was it "meh, don't care for him," or "I hate him and want to kill him?" And how many players were "not everyone?" Did my list of suspects just grow exponentially?

I was totally going to have to get Charles here. Hmm. I had a plan, but it might take more than one ghost. It was time to call in the cavalry.

CHAPTER 11

The next morning after getting ready for work, I had about ten minutes to check in with Charles. I stood next to the kitchen table. "Charles, please come."

He appeared next to me, smiling. "Good morning, Avery."

"You're in a good mood. What's going on?"

His smile widened into a grin. "I helped Sergeant Fox solve an art theft case from fifty years ago. I was actually going to ask if you could maybe stumble upon the clues and nudge Bellamy towards the answer."

I blew out a breath. Every time I did something like this, I risked people finding out I thought I could talk to ghosts. Well... I *could* talk to ghosts; it's just that they'd think I was delusional. "I'll need to know the details before I agree to anything." Which also reminded me that I was chasing up the pirate's case, but that would have to wait now that I was helping Bellamy with Adam's murder. "Today's also not a good day. Bellamy's under the pump, and I have to interview someone for an article this morning. Can we deal with this another day?"

He put his hands on his hips and huffed. "Fine. The first case I solve with Fox, and you're not enthusiastic."

I frowned. Letting people down sucked. "I'm sorry, Charles. I'm super proud of you. I hope you know that. But real-world things sometimes can't wait. What if we talk about it in a few days? There's a lot of stuff crowding my brain at the moment, and I don't think I can give your case the attention it deserves right now. Is that okay?"

He dropped his arms to his sides. "Fine." His tone was so child-like that I had to bite my bottom lip to keep from laughing. I had a feeling that would make him feel like I didn't take him seriously. "Why did you call me?"

"I have a favour to ask, although I'm sure you'll enjoy it. I was wondering if you and Sergeant Fox can help me with Bellamy's case? I need someone to listen in on conversations at the rugby club, see if you can find out anything for me. I'm going to go there when they next have practice and be obvious that I'm there to talk about Adam for the paper. I'm hoping that'll encourage people to say things to each other that they wouldn't say in front of me." I told him about Adam's girlfriend, the coach's assistant, and the guy I spoke to yesterday afternoon, plus the one who wouldn't speak. "Those two guys are probably more important and more likely to say something. But if anyone there looks uncomfortable, I would love for you or Fox to be listening in. Will you do that for me?"

He wore a thoughtful expression. "That sounds like fun, I suppose. I'll talk to Sergeant Fox about it. When do you need to know?"

"Tomorrow would be great."

"Okay, done. Is that it?"

"Yes, thanks. I'll see you around. And congrats again on the crime solving." I smiled.

He smiled back. "Thanks, Avery. Bye." He waved, then disappeared.

Time to go to work.

Sixty-five-year-old identical twins Beryl and Beverly still lived together, had the same grey hair pulled back in a bun, wore the same sequined silver leotard with white tights, and had the same amount of cellulite from what I could see, and I could see way, way too much. No one should wear white tights with nothing over the top. No one. Neither of the women had married, and I couldn't help but wonder if it was because they had a propensity for wearing see-through tights.

I was covering their story because they'd entered a local dancing eisteddfod, and they thought if they gained some popularity before they competed, the judges would be more favourable.

"We're up against people half our age." Beryl looked at Beverly for confirmation. Or was that Beverly looking at Beryl? They were as identical as two people could be. Beryl had introduced both of them when I came in, but they'd moved around the room like two magician's cups while I'd been here, and now I had no idea which one was the cup with the ball. Neither wore jewellery, and their shoes were the same too. Oh no. Those shoes were tap shoes. Their hallway had carpet, and the clicking as they'd come into this room didn't register because I was doing my best to remember who was who, but I'd failed at that anyway, so maybe I should've been paying more attention. Tap was my least favourite of all the dancing styles. It was lots of clickety clacking about nothing.

The other one said, "They don't know how good we are though, do they, Beryl?" Ah, phew. Thank you, Beverly. Now, if I could put nametags on them without offending them, I'd do it.

"Not in the least. That trophy is ours." She tapped her feet in some kind of dance move and grinned, revealing red lipstick clinging doggedly to her front tooth. Full stage make-up was no trouble for these ladies, even though it wasn't performance day. I didn't have the heart to tell them the thick powder accentuated their wrinkles.

"How long have you both been dancing?" I held my pen at the ready.

Beverly broke into a quick clickety-clack for five seconds, which was five seconds too long. She finished with a flourish of her arms. "Since we were ten."

I had to give it to them, though. That was commitment. "Wow, that's a long time. Will you be the oldest competitors?"

Beverly gave her sister a quick look, then turned back to me. "Yes. We usually are. But we've got more energy and stamina than women half our age. Isn't that right, Ber?" Beverly stomped her feet for a few quick beats and ended with a high kick that I only just dodged. Maybe they should've set up a stage for this interview.

Beryl nodded enthusiastically. "Yes. We're always full of beans." She tapped out the identical ditty her sister had, but I was ready, so I shuffled backwards, way out of kicking range. Did they need to punctuate every statement with a dance move? It would be a great way to lose weight.

"Do you have friends or family who will support you on performance day?" I liked to throw in serious questions, even if the subject matter was a bit... unusual. It was always good to get to know the people behind the stories.

Beverly smiled. "Oh, yes. Our niece and nephew come to see us with their little ones." This must be a particularly joyous thing for them because Beverly did a quick tappity tap, then a cartwheel, narrowly missing the couch on the far side of the room.

Beryl clapped. "Nicely executed, Bev!" Then it was her turn. Instead of doing a cartwheel, her arms flung wide, and she tapped while spinning. The breeze was nice.

Having them dance every time they commented was a deterrent to me asking questions, but I didn't have enough information for an article. Argh. "How do you usually go at your competitions?"

Beverly tappity tapped all the way to a bookcase filled with trophies. She elegantly floated her arm towards the display. "Ta da! We win or place quite often, although we haven't done that for four years. But I have a good feeling about this eisteddfod." She spun, spun, spun towards her sister and stopped. "Isn't that right, Ber?"

Beryl nodded and grinned. Thankfully she didn't say anything and kept still.

"I'd like to take some video for the article because we'll show it on the internet."

"Ooh, that's so exciting." Beryl clapped and tapped for a few seconds. I bit back my grin. They *were* pretty cute.

They put their heads close and whispered. When they were done, Beverly looked at me. "We're not going to show you what we're doing for next week—if anyone sees, they might steal our routine. Instead, we'll perform the sugarplum fairy."

I wasn't into ballet either—although if I were into any dancing, that wouldn't be a bad one to be into—but I was pretty sure sugarplum fairies didn't clack or stomp. This oughta be good.

Beverly pressed Play on an old-style tape recorder. Tinny classical music bounced off the room's hard surfaces. I cringed. If I didn't have a headache before this performance, I was certainly going to have one after. Beverly and her sister stood next to each other, and one of them said, "Five, six, seven, eight…" Simultaneously, they took off with rapid, tiny steps, the sound reminiscent of a herd of possums galumphing across a metal roof at night. Clackety chaos.

They threw their arms up elegantly as if they were fairies flying, which was at horrendous odds with the flurry of noise assaulting my ears. Could this be over now? Imagine paying to see this. Yikes.

Oops. I remembered to press Record on the video.

I had to admit that the ending was spectacular. Beryl—or was it Beverly?— ran and jumped into the other one's arms and was promptly lofted overhead and held there for a good five seconds while the song finished. Their grins as one sister set the other down strong-armed a grin out of me. Look how happy they were. I pressed Stop on the recording and clapped. "Well done. That lift at the end was impressive!" I meant what I said. If I tried to do that with someone who weighed the same as me, I would collapse and kill both of us. Not to mention they were in their sixties.

They bowed with another arm flourish.

"I'll get one picture of you two standing together smiling." They put an arm around each other's waists, their outside arms held up in a dancer's pose while they beamed. *Click.* "Great. Thank you. And good luck with your competition. I'm sure you'll slay them."

"Thank you, darling. I'm sure we will. Thanks for coming to see us today. We hope you enjoyed our performance."

It was times like this that even the most honest, kind person had to admit that lying had its merits. "I did. It was fantastic."

"You should come and watch us perform! It would be lovely to see you there." At this point, I wasn't even trying to guess who was speaking.

"Oh, thanks for the invite. If I'm free, I'll definitely come." Did an angel lose their wings every time I lied? There'd be no angels left by the time I died.

"We hope to see you there."

I bade them goodbye and hurried out of there. One could only lie so much in one day. It had to be bad for my complexion or something.

When I returned to the office, there was no Adam waiting for me. I smiled. That banishing thing really worked. But, from what Celeste said, he'd be back again in the evening—twenty-four hours or so after I'd banished him. I could just oust him again, I supposed.

Carina and Finnegan were at their desks, arguing about something. Carina was the first to notice me as I plonked my bag on my desk. "Ah, she's here. You can settle d'is for us."

I chuckled. "Happy to."

Finnegan narrowed his eyes at me. "That's not fair. Avery'll take your side for sure." He pointed to me, then Carina and back again. "You women stick together."

In my previous life, no women stuck with me... at least not Brad's friends. I was always on my own when it came to sticking up for myself. I pushed the depressing thought aside. "I'll be impartial. Promise."

Finnegan rolled his eyes, and Carina gave a firm nod. "Okay, Avery, so, Finny here t'inks d'at marzipan is lovely. I say it's disgusting. What do you t'ink?"

I gagged. "Marzipan is disgusting. You're welcome to any I might come across, Vinegar."

He huffed. "I told you you'd stick together."

This was obviously a stupid argument, but still, it needed to be settled. "As much as I think Carina is awesome, if she'd said she loved marzipan, I would've disagreed. Seriously, I'll eat almost anything, but that's where I draw the line. Next time you have a disagreement, consult me again, and I'll probably take your side, Vinegar. As long as it's not about marzipan's virtues, because there are none."

"Stitched up, as usual. If anyone wants me, bad luck. I've got work to do." I was pretty sure he was fake sulking because it was a stupid argument and how could anyone get upset over that? Carina laughed, and she didn't have a malicious bone in her body as far as I could tell, so it must mean it was all a bit of fun. I would've confirmed, but then I'd look like an idiot for worrying so much. But what if he was upset? Argh! Whatever. If he was angry with me, I'd find out about it later when he ignored me.

I sat and set my laptop up. I wanted to knock over that article ASAP, then do more research on the pirate's family. Come to think of it, I should've asked Celeste about curses. I was still on the fence —logical Avery said, "don't be stupid," but Avery who knew about ghosts said, "if there's ghosts, maybe there are curses." It might just be that Burgess's family made bad decisions, and sometimes when luck pushed you down, it kept you there. Some situations or cycles were hard to escape from. Yet again, I marvelled at how being struck by lightning was the best thing that could've happened to me. If I hadn't been able to see ghosts, I'd probably still be living with abusive Brad and be putting up with my horrible parents. How long would I have gone before realising that life could be so much better and leaving? Maybe never. Such a sobering thought.

Just as I finished reading through my article for the second time, a young woman, dressed in black jeans and black long-sleeve T-shirt, stood at the open door and knocked. She was tall, maybe five ten, and slim—almost too slim. An air of frailty clung to her. It was in the hollow of her cheeks and in the way her back hunched slightly as she finished knocking and hugged herself. Her pale skin sharply contrasted against her dark hair, which fell just past her shoulders in a bob with a side part that allowed her hair to fall across her face, covering at least half of it. There was something familiar about her as she gazed across the room at Finnegan.

Her timid voice would've barely made it across the room. "Hey, Finny."

His head shot up, his gaze immediately finding her. He jumped out of his chair and strode to the doorway. "Hannah!" He gently hugged her as if he was worried he'd break her. "What are you doing here?" His voice held curiosity.

"A girl can visit her big brother, can't she?" Wow, his sister. That's why she looked so familiar. She had the same eye shape, hair colour, and straight nose as her brother, but he wasn't anywhere near as pale, and his level of confidence was worlds different to hers.

He grinned, but I could see the wariness in his eyes. "Of course. Always. Do you want to come in and have a seat, or do you want to go for coffee?"

Her gaze briefly touched me before flitting to Carina and back to Finnegan. I was staying as still as possible so as not to startle her. "Can we go for coffee?"

"Of course. I'll just grab my phone."

While Finnegan did that, I smiled at Hannah and made my voice as gentle as possible. "Hi, Hannah. I'm Avery. Nice to meet you."

She blinked, and she said nothing for a beat but recovered. "Hi, Avery. Nice to meet you too." Her eye contact was brief before she shyly turned her head to watch her brother cross the room back to her.

Finnegan gave me a small smile, then put his hand on his sister's lower back. "Let's go get a cuppa. Are you still into peppermint tea?" She nodded but was quiet as they walked out.

Carina and I looked at each other. She waggled her brows, and I took it to mean she wanted to talk about what just happened. I rose and went to the door, poking my head out to check they'd gone. Yep. I grabbed Finnegan's chair and turned it towards Carina, then sat. "So, what's the story?" Argh, I felt like such a gossip, which was something I didn't like. Gossiping was puerile and rarely constructive, but this was more to find out about Finnegan. He was definitely like an onion when it came to getting to know him. He rarely got personal.

"Well, d'at's only d'e second time she's come here. She normally doesn't leave d'e house. She still lives with d'eir parents in London, and she doesn't work. She's painfully shy."

"I picked up on that. Is she okay? She... doesn't look healthy." Maybe she had a chronic illness?

"I t'ink she's okay, but you're right—she looks under d'e wead'er. Finny doesn't say much about her, but I know she went t'rough a difficult time a few years ago. He wouldn't spill on the details d'ough. Based on what I do know, her turning up here by herself is a big t'ing."

He'd been so sweet with her. He seemed like a decent guy—as long as you didn't expect to settle down with him—but he was more than decent with his sister. He looked so happy to see her, and he'd been so gentle with her. What would it be like to have someone care about you that much? I didn't know, and I doubted I ever would. At least I had my life and myself. That would have to be enough... and it was. Every day I was grateful for having survived the lightning strike. I wasn't going to ruin my second chance pining after something that was unlikely to ever happen. Me loving me would have to be enough. I'd make sure of it.

"She seemed nice."

"Yeah, she did. Anyway, I hope you're wrong... about her being ill." She twirled a section of her blue hair around her finger. "Oh, and t'anks for backing me up before. Do you really hate marzipan?"

I chuckled. "Yes. Definitely. My most-hated food ever."

She laughed. "I wasn't sure if you were just trying to annoy him. I was, by d'e way." She winked. "I hate marzipan, too, but I know d'at he loves it." She sighed. "I s'ppose I'd better get back to work. Ah, if only d'e bills would pay d'emselves."

"I hear you."

Back to work we went. Once I'd sent the article off to Macpherson, I rang and arranged another interview for tomorrow, with a local lady who made candles. That should be a fairly normal interview, at least. A little voice inside my head said, *Don't be too sure about that.* I ignored it. If I listened to that voice every time, I'd lose all hope.

Now that I had some spare time, I was going to look into William's case, which meant a thorough online search was in order. I also wanted to go back to Exeter, to the library. They were sure to have books on the region's history. Any information would help my investigation at this point. If only William had kept in touch with where his descendants went. But I supposed the number of people he would've had to keep track of would be ridiculous, and if he'd never met them, why would he care? I didn't even care what happened to my living relatives… except for my sister. And if that didn't make me sound horrible, I didn't know what did. We were all a product of our upbringing in some ways, whether we wanted to acknowledge that or not.

I drove Daisy home and parked her in the premium spot. Chuckling as I got out, I praised myself for my good timing. Finnegan was going to grumble when he got home. He he. It was the little things.

As I exited the laneway, an excited voice called out, "Avery! Long time no see."

I stopped and turned to my right. "Josie. Hello." I smiled at my across-the-way neighbour. She was Mrs Crabby's polar opposite—where one was grumpy, the other was cheery. Where one kept to herself, the other jumped on any chance to say hello. Where one had a dismal front garden of weeds and dirt (that I suspected matched her soul), the other's garden was awash with colour—a vibrant work of art that cheered me up every time I saw it. I wandered over to her. "How have you been? Sorry I haven't ducked around, but I've had a lot on." That was partly the truth. The other reason was that I was still wary. Yes, I'd made friends since I'd been here, but that was reluctantly. Trust remained a difficult undertaking, and I was always ready to expect the worst from people I got close to. Limiting those numbers was for my benefit, but sometimes, you couldn't help but be sucked into someone's orbit. Josie was one of those people, and I was quickly losing my battle of aloofness.

She touched my arm. "Wait here, lovie. I've got something for you." She turned and hurried inside. Her waddling walk didn't slow her down at all. Was she off to grab some of her homegrown produce? Two weeks ago, she'd given me some tomatoes and cucumbers. Super delicious. It made me consider starting my own vegie patch, but then I thought about Mrs Crabby and her objections—because there would've been many—and I quickly dropped the idea.

Thunder rumbled in the distance. I turned and stared at the sky. Charcoal clouds drifted across the azure backdrop. The sky was clear above Manesbury, but it would be pouring in approximately ten minutes if my weather radar was any indication.

Josie came back out, a plastic container in her hands. She smiled and handed it to me. "My famous black forest torte."

"Oh, wow, that looks delish. But I can't eat a whole cake by myself." Well, I probably could, but it would take a few days, and it wouldn't do my waistline any good.

"Maybe invite someone over for coffee or tea?" She glanced at Finnegan's place, then waggled her brows.

Argh. I pasted a smile on my face. Two could play at that game. "Sharing? That's a great idea!"

She covered her momentary surprise with a grin and clap. "I thought so. You could do with a strapping young man taking care of you."

I swallowed my urge to say that I could take care of myself and was actually doing a bang-up job of it, but instead, I played my ace. "I'm going to take this cake to work tomorrow. That way, I can share it with Finnegan *and* Carina. They are so going to love you. I can't wait to have some. Maybe I'll sneak a piece tonight." I grinned, which was genuine. My tastebuds were already spurting saliva at the thought.

She peered at me. "I don't think you're getting my meaning."

My voice was kind when I said, "Oh, I do, but I'm happy with my life as it is."

"For now." Wow, she was insistent.

"Yes, for now." *Possibly for always.* "Besides, I have cake. Who could ask for anything more?" I waggled my brows.

She chuckled. "You got me there, lovie. Okay, I'll stop needling you now. You enjoy that cake."

"I will." A thought popped into my head, and I said something before I could change my mind and be a turtle. "I'm going to Exeter tomorrow. Do you need anything?"

"Thanks for asking, but I'm good. Got everything I need right here." She gave a nod to her cottage. I wanted to point out that I felt the same about my place and life, but she was only trying to be nice, so I kept it to myself.

"Not a problem. But if you ever need anything, let me know."

"Thanks, Avery. You're such a dear. Well, enjoy that cake, and tell Finnegan I said hello." She winked, turned, and walked towards her house. I laughed to myself and went home. I had more important things to think about than Finnegan, and that suited me just fine.

CHAPTER 12

Friday morning, and I didn't even get a chance to get out of bed before I had my answer from Charles about listening in on the rugby players. "Psst, Avery. Wake up."

I cracked my eyes open. "What time is it?"

"How should I know?" He disappeared, reappearing a few seconds later. "The sun's up, but it's early."

"And you're waking me up because?" The lack of urgency in his demeanour meant that at least there was no emergency, not like the time he woke me up because he was worried about Mr Donigal.

"Sergeant Fox is keen to help with your case. He's worried about Sergeant Bellamy. He doesn't want him demoted because he said he's good at his job."

I sat up. "He is, and he's a nice enough person. I hate the guy who was killed, and I'd rather not help him, but...." Was he evil enough to deserve being murdered? Probably not, but it didn't mean I had to want to help him. And I got the sense that there wasn't a serial killer on the loose. The only urgency I felt with this case was for Bellamy's job.

"Yeah, I know. Sometimes we have to do things we don't want to do because it's for the greater good."

I grinned. "Yes." I was sure I'd said something similar to him when I wanted him to face his fears and sort his life out... well, his death? Anyway, it must have sunk in because he was throwing my words back at me. "Yes we do. So, tomorrow afternoon, do you and Sergeant Fox want to come in the car with me? That way, I can call for you here before I leave. It might be easier."

He shrugged. "Whatever. Either way is good. I guess if you drive us there, we can talk about what you want us to do."

"Excellent. Thanks, Charles. So, what else is going on?"

"Meh, nothing much. I'm going to visit a friend now. I'll see you tomorrow."

"Okay. Bye, Charles."

And he was gone. Just like that. I picked my phone up off the bedside table. Argh, it was early. Only seven. I could've slept in till eight, but I was wide awake now. Might as well go for a warm-up jog and get some hapkido practice in.

Big. Mistake.

As soon as I got to the laneway, my least favourite ghost in the world appeared in front of me. I ran through him. Hades. No rock. Grrr.

He followed, easily keeping up with my medium jogging pace. "So, you do like me. You've been looking into my murder. I know because people around the club have been talking."

Breathe in, one two three; breathe out. "Argh. I do not like you. The complete opposite, actually."

"Me thinks she doth protest too much. You sound like those women who pretend they don't want it after they've clearly been begging for it all night. Women love a man who takes control."

I stopped dead. Anger exploded through my veins. The nerve of this sicko. My gaze bore through him. Helping Bellamy had kick-started my motivation on this, but Adam had dialled it right up. I wouldn't stop until the crime was solved, and I wanted to do it as quickly as possible. "You're a sick piece of work; you know that? And guess what? I am going to solve your murder so you can get closure and go to hell. Literally. That's where you're going. Those women didn't want you any more than you would've wanted a broken back. Whoever killed you did the world a favour." I pivoted around, leaving him standing there, mouth agape, and ran home. This guy brought out the worst in me. Hatred spurred my feet. The longer I engaged with this toxic soul, the worse I'd feel later. I didn't stop running until I was safely inside my locked apartment. Mrs Crabby had called after me to not stomp up the stairs, but I didn't answer since it was after I closed my door.

What to do? If I grabbed my rock... oops, crystal... I wouldn't want to offend Celeste by accidentally calling it a rock. If I grabbed my rockish-looking *crystal* and went outside, I'd have to say stuff, and I might look weird to Mrs Crabby who would surely be watching. I could take my phone out there, but she'd wonder why I wasn't on the phone in the apartment. I could fake it and say the signal was dodgy upstairs. The other option was to wait until I went to work, and just get him then.

I walked to the window and stared out. Adam paced up and down in front of the fence. Back and forth, back and forth. If only I could call Finnegan to come and get rid of him, but Adam was a ghost, and Finnegan would be useless in this situation. I sighed. The only person I could rely on right now was myself. And wasn't this what I wanted—independence? *There you go, Avery, independence. Doesn't it feel great?*

I rubbed my arms to dislodge the goosebumps. Time for some stretching, maybe push-ups and sit-ups, then coffee. After I was done with all that, I got changed and checked out the window again. Adam was gone, although that didn't mean he wasn't there. He could be floating above my roof.

As much as I hated confrontation, I was ready for him. When I walked out of the house with my bag over my shoulder, I held my phone in one hand and the crystal in the other. *Come and get it, buddy.*

But he really was gone.

When I made it to the main road without being accosted, I breathed out my relief. The house I was going to was on the other side of Manesbury, about five minutes from the office, and since the clouds were languid and white, I didn't need to worry about rain.

Ms Oatlands lived in a quaint stone bungalow with a low stone fence and straight pathway that led me through colourful summer flowers to the front porch. A ceramic plaque of a cute house martin hung on a nail in the brick next to the doorbell. We didn't have those in Australia as far as I knew, but when I'd pointed one out to Carina, she'd told me what it was. I did love animals. They were nothing like people, had no agenda except survival, but they were full of affection for no other reason than they adored their people.

I knocked, and the door opened. Wow, that was quick. Had she been watching me walk up the path? A vertically challenged, rotund woman with short greying hair and thick glasses smiled up at me. She reminded me of the fairy godmother in the original animated Disney movie *Cinderella*, but younger, maybe about sixty. Cute. Her voice was high and added to the effect. "Hello, dear one. You must be Avery."

I smiled. "I am. And you must be Ms Oatlands. It's lovely to meet you." I held out my hand.

She pushed it out of the way and stepped in for a hug. "None of that formal nonsense. We hug around here." This was very... non-British. They were normally rather untouchy feely with people they didn't know. Okay, so my friends hadn't been. Maybe that assumption was wrong? Or maybe it was true for the upper class rather than the working class. I'd have to ask Meg about it. Anyway, I wasn't touchy feely, so the hug was uncomfortable. It was confronting to be squashed against her ample, warm bosom. At least I was taller, and my face was clear of the fray. She finally released me and beckoned me inside. "Let's go through to my studio."

Her home smelled faintly of cinnamon, but an undercurrent of disquiet had the hairs on my nape standing on end. It wasn't until we'd traversed the hall and living area and exited into the small, rectangular backyard that I discovered what it was.

A pale man stood next to the small green shed that abutted the back fence. I wasn't touching my ghost-finding rock... ah, crystal, but seeing as how Ms Oatlands didn't so much as glance at him, I could assume he was a ghost. His wide-eyed stare gave me goosebumps. He shook his head, then glared at Ms Oatlands. His pointed finger sheared the air as he stabbed it towards her. Then he ran at the stubby woman but disappeared before reaching her. How strange. What in Hades was all that about?

The shed door creaked as my host opened it. "Here's where the magic happens." She ushered me inside. Something crunched under my shoes on the timber floor. When I looked down, I discovered it wasn't dirt. Small white dots stood out against the dark floor. Sand or salt? "Is everything all right, Avery?"

I jerked my gaze to the candlemaker. "Oh, yes. Sorry. I hope I haven't brought sand into your shed." I knew it wasn't me, but I didn't want to accuse her of having a dirty studio.

She smiled. "Oh, that. It's salt. I spilled a packet the other day and mustn't have cleaned it up properly. So, what do you think?" She waved an arm at the workbench and shelves behind her. "The cloudier yellow ones are beeswax."

I picked up one of the thick, round candles and sniffed. "Smells lovely." I placed it back on the bench and peered closer at the other wax creations. "That sausage dog is cute."

"They're one of my bestsellers."

"Do you have a mould, or do you carve it out?" I really had no idea about how to make candles, but I had watched a brief video last night to make sure I had some familiarity with it. Mostly, candles were poured into moulds, but maybe the more artistic candlemakers were sculptors.

"Both. The sausage dogs are moulds, but this one here"—she picked up a green-and-yellow candle in the shape of a pineapple— "I carved. There are some finishes you just can't get from a mould. It's also useful for when you want layers of colour to show through." She picked up another thick, long, orange candle. Complicated geometric shapes, stars, and hearts had been cut into it, revealing a purple underlayer.

"This looks kind of witchy." I chuckled. "I can imagine it sitting next to a bubbling cauldron." Yes, I knew ghosts existed, and even though I wasn't willing to believe magic did, people did practice witchcraft. Whether it eventuated in any actual outcomes or not was another thing.

Her expression settled into contemplation. "You're very observant. Do you practice wicca?"

"Oh, no. I'm more of a… realist."

The raised eyebrow was a giveaway that I'd just insulted her. Oops. Then she smiled. "Don't knock it till you've tried it." She winked.

"Do you practice it?"

She picked up her carved candle and slid her fingertips over the shapes. "I've been known to." She put the candle down and looked at me. "But you're not here to talk about that. Why don't I show you some more of my artwork."

I took a few photos and asked about her methods, then I videoed her making one of the simpler candles in a mould. When we were done, she offered me a red candle with dark flecks. On closer inspection, the flecks revealed themselves to be bugs. Was that fly staring at me? Also, ew. When the candle burned down, would the insect burn or just drop out of the melty wax?

"Do you like it?"

I was careful to keep my opinions out of my expression. "Um… yes. It's… different." *Come on, Avery, think of something positive to say.* "I love the colour." *Yay, you did it!* And under very trying circumstances. I didn't have quite enough for my article, so it was time to ask a couple more questions. "What do your family think about your work?"

She stopped caressing a dragon candle and looked at me. "I'm estranged from my parents, and I'm an only child. My husband left me two Christmases ago without any warning and without so much as a goodbye." She gave me an awkward half smile.

"I'm so sorry."

Her head tilted to one side, and she sighed. "At least I have my candles and my magic. They both give me such comfort and pleasure."

"Oh, that's good. You're obviously a brave and resilient person."

Hopefully those compliments would make her feel better. This stuff wasn't what I wanted to focus on in the article though. I could be so unempathetic. At least it was only in my own head so I was the only person who knew how rubbish I really was. "Would you like to pick your favourite two candles and hold them so I can get a picture? Just stand in front of the shelves." I smiled. A change of subject was as good as a holiday... okay, maybe not, but it was all I had.

She smiled. "Of course." She picked up the dragon and a green frog. Totally adorable. They were things I would consider buying for myself, if I were into knickknacks. But I wasn't. "Smile." She smiled. I took the photo. And we were done. "We're all finished. Thank you so much for inviting me into your studio."

"My pleasure, dear. Thank you for coming. When will you be featuring me?"

"I'm not sure, but it will either be this afternoon or tomorrow. Just keep an eye out."

"Will do."

I turned to leave. My gaze hit the floor, just behind the doorway. Was that a line of salt? Is that what had crunched under my feet when I first came in? Salt supposedly kept evil spirits and ghosts out of the house. But from what I'd learned, generally, it wasn't easy for them to gain access unless they were invited. It had certainly kept my place free of unwanted spirits. But.... My eyes widened as I stepped out and realisation hit.

It wasn't just the salt that alerted me.

The ghost from earlier stood in front of me, and I walked through him. Chills cascaded along my arms and back, and I shuddered. But I didn't stop walking. His voice chased after me. "She killed me. Adriana killed me."

Possum poo. I made sure to look at the floor on the inside of the back doorway to the house, and sure enough, there was salt. It made sense—she didn't want her dead husband to come into his own house. He could gain access without an invitation, so in order to keep him out, she'd had to resort to salt.

I was totally going to hell, but just before I exited the front door,

I stopped and turned. "Um, Ms Oatlands, can I ask you a personal question? This isn't for the article. It's for me."

She clasped her hands in front of herself. "Yes. I obviously reserve the right to not answer it, but go ahead."

If I had a dollar for every lie I'd told…. "Well, my fiancé left me recently, and he was abusive." Okay, so it was kind of true, we just weren't engaged. "I was wondering if your husband was too. I don't know if you have any good advice on how to avoid men like that, but if you do, I'm all ears." If I could get any information about her husband at all, I could decide whether to gather more evidence. It wasn't my place to decide who was punished and who wasn't, but if he'd made her suffer and she was just defending herself, who was I to send the police to arrest her and make her life hell all over again? On the other hand, if she was a cold-blooded murderer, I was definitely going to do more research and put my own letter for the dead in the paper on the husband's behalf. I could go to Bellamy with that, and he'd at least listen. The other option was making up some kind of story and say during my visit I'd become suspicious. I had no idea what that would look like though, and it would be easier to get caught out. Not for the first time, I wished that if I told people I saw ghosts, they'd believe me.

She gently grabbed my forearm. "I'm so sorry to hear this. I'm afraid he wasn't abusive. Rather, he wasn't supportive at all. He made fun of my candle making, said I shouldn't waste time with that hobby, and don't get me started on what he thought about me being a witch. He laughed at me a few times. I told him he should leave, and one day, he finally did. I heard he took up with a woman in London, but who knows? If he was as annoying to her as he was to me, they're probably no longer together." She released my arm and smiled. "I was upset at first, but I soon got used to being in my own space. It's rather peaceful now. I'm not sure how you can avoid annoying men except by staying single. Honestly, it's a lovely way to live."

If she was telling the truth, those weren't horrible things. Maybe they weren't compatible, but that wasn't a reason to kill someone. Challenge accepted.

A FROZEN STIFF

It was time to put my pirate friend's story on the backburner because now I had a second, recent murder to help with. Well, not help with, but you know… help solve. Except no one else knew about this one. I had a bit more research to complete before I was satisfied that's what happened, so I supposed I'd better get started.

CHAPTER 13

W hen I returned to the empty office, I wrote the article on Ms Oatlands and her candles. As soon as that was emailed to Macpherson, I googled "Adriana Oatlands husband missing." Only one hit came up. A blog post by a Sandra Smith. Her blog was called "Single and Smashing it." Other articles included, "Dinner for One Can be Fun" and "Five Ways to Kill Time When You're Lonely." Ha, maybe I should follow it. Which reminded me about the cake. Doh! In the stress of the morning and my hurry to get to my car without being bothered, I'd forgotten to bring the cake. Sure, I could go home and get it, but I was too lazy for that. Oh well, looked like I'd have to eat it by myself (*SorryNot-Sorry*) and hope Josie didn't ask me about it. If I managed to avoid her for a couple of weeks, maybe she'd forget about it.

The blog post with Ms Oatlands was about her experiences after her husband "left" her. She said she missed him but had made a peaceful home where she gets "to do what I want when I want without any annoying nattering." My forehead wrinkled. The article was written a year and a half ago—approximately a month after he "left" her after twenty-one years of marriage. No, I couldn't speak for everyone or her specifically, but wouldn't it take longer to adjust if your husband up and left you without a word? It didn't prove anything, but I made a note in a new document under the heading Alarm Bells.

Second fact in the article that had my spidey senses tingling was that she spoke about building the shed and doing her candles as a my-husband-left-me gift to herself to cheer herself up since he'd never allowed her to have her own studio for it before. Was he buried under the shed?

I copied and pasted the blog link into my document, then screenshotted everything in the post in case she twigged I was sniffing around. Not that she would have any idea, but you never knew, and I didn't want this evidence to disappear.

After that, I checked voting records. Her husband's name was Earl, and he was registered at an address in Ealing, London. I wrote it down. Then I logged into our database of births, deaths, and marriages. There was no death recorded for Earl Oatlands around that Christmas. When I googled his name, all that came up was a couple of mentions of him winning wood-carving competitions. Huh? Why would he complain about her candles if he was creative as well? Was he a narcissist or something? I added that to my list. Right. I had what I needed to continue my search. I wasn't going to interview anyone for Adam's case until Saturday, so I had time. Earl deserved help, and after seeing how upset he was, I couldn't not look into it. Yes, I had a lot of work to do, but you know what they said about what to do if you wanted something done—give it to a busy person. But first, I was going to grab lunch.

When I got back to the office, I looked up the address Earl had supposedly moved to. Huh? It was a St Andrews Church. That didn't sound right. I called them and spoke to a woman called Dotty. She said she'd never heard of Earl Oatlands. His description didn't ring a bell either. That wasn't unexpected since he was dead. His claims of being murdered seemed to be true.

After more research, I discovered he hadn't been married before and had no children. But did he have any siblings or parents that were alive? It would be so much easier if I could talk to his ghost again. I could easily make up a story about the photos not working out or something, but I would rather be there without Ms Oatlands present. There was no way I could ask Earl a question with her listening. Ooh, I could ask Charles to— Ah, no I couldn't. He wouldn't be able to go onto the property. But was Earl trapped, or could he walk free? It wouldn't surprise me if Ms Oatlands had spelled him there. And, yes, now I was believing in witchcraft. If that salt worked, which it seemed to because he hadn't followed us inside and he'd wanted to talk to me, then maybe she could trap him in the yard too.

I looked up birth records via our office account and wrote down his parents' names. Then I looked up their records. Both deceased. He had a brother, Tom, who didn't have an English address. I couldn't find any death records, but as far as English records were concerned, he didn't live here. Which meant he could be anywhere. I got onto Facebook and looked up Tom Oatlands. There were a handful but none of the right age. I then looked up Ms Oatlands, but her account was set to private, and I couldn't even see who her friends were.

I really, really needed to speak to Earl. How I would do that, well, I had no idea. What was weird was that there were no missing person's posts on the internet. No one saying "have you seen this man?" Surely he'd had friends or a job, people who didn't trust his wife or knew he wouldn't just up and leave without saying anything? How come no one had reported him missing? If they had, the police couldn't just take his wife's word for the fact that he left, could they? I would love to ask Bellamy about it, but he'd ask why I was concerned. I didn't have an answer I could use... yet. I'd have to work on that as well. But back to the potential job. I needed to find out if he'd worked and if so where? She was estranged from her parents, from what she said. Maybe they could answer my questions and it wouldn't get back to her? That could work. By the time I walked home, I had a plan.

As I exited the laneway, Josie called out to me. "Avery! You have some explaining to do." Bummer. I quickly sighed, plastered a smile on my face, then stopped and turned. Double bummer—Finnegan stood with her, an evil grin on his face. Damn him. Stupid neighbours with their silly ideas and interfering cakes.

"Hi, Josie. Vinegar. How is everyone?"

Finnegan tsked. "I hear you were meant to share cake. Why did I miss out?"

I wasn't even going to play coy. Today had been tiring, and I didn't have it in me. "I just had a stressful morning, and I rushed out. I forgot. Sorry."

His eyes widened. I was assuming it was because he didn't expect me to apologise rather than it being because I forgot. His surprise dissipated. He smiled. "I don't suppose it was because you ate it all already?"

I chuckled. "If only. I admit to having one piece, which was maybe a big one, but there's plenty left. Would you like me to bring it over, and we can all go inside and have some?" I nodded towards Josie's front door.

Josie cocked her head to the side. "Oh, I'm so sorry. I have to go out. Why don't you two run along. I'm sure you can have tea and cake at your place, Avery." Her triumphant smile made me want to sigh, but I held it in. *Yay me.*

Finnegan, with his sixth sense into how to annoy me, grinned. "I would love that! Lead the way, Lightning."

"Have fun, you two." Josie grinned, turned, and hurried inside. Seriously? My face heated. The way she was behaving, Finnegan was going to think I was into him. Okay, so I was, but I didn't want anything to come of it, least of all me looking like some lovesick desperado.

Time to address the elephant in the street. "I don't know why, but she has visions of matchmaking us, I'm sure. Sorry about that. You're welcome to cake and tea or coffee. Just don't get any ideas."

"Are you normally this welcoming, or is it just me?" He chuckled.

I grinned. "It's just you." Argh, he was being funny and charming. I could hardly be mean. "Come on, then. If I eat it all by myself, I won't fit into my clothes."

He held his hands up, his eyes glinting with mischief. "I'm not saying anything."

"Wise man. Come on, then."

Halfway across the road to my place, Adam appeared. Crud. He gave Finnegan the once over and sniggered. "He looks emo. What a joke. You slutting around, gorgeous? And by the way, you have no taste. What would any woman want with a wussy office worker?"

Oh. My. God. I slid my hand into my bag and felt around for my crystals. The banishment one was bigger and rougher than the other one, so it wasn't hard to tell which was which. I gripped it as we reached my gate.

Finnegan shivered and looked at the sky, then at me. "Has the temperature dropped?"

I did my best to ignore Adam who was trying to punch Finnegan in the head. My heart rate had kicked up—my body knew something was off. "I think so. Feels colder, doesn't it. A nice cup of tea or coffee will fix it."

He opened the gate for me. "After you."

I smiled, despite Adam scowling at both Finnegan and me and anger sparking off him. If only I could think the banishment words rather than say them. Fingers crossed that solving the murder would mean I'd be free of him. "Thanks." I hurried to the door and unlocked it, the chill only leaving when we were both safely inside, the door shut. It wasn't till we were standing in my apartment alone that a different kind of nervousness set it. Of course, I would be the only one to feel it. It wasn't like Finnegan wanted anything but cake from me.

Without making eye contact, I said, "Sit wherever. I'll put the kettle on." I dumped my bag on the kitchen table and crossed to the electric kettle. Unfortunately, he chose the kitchen table to sit at. Why couldn't he sit on the couch? "English breakfast or Earl Grey? Or would you prefer coffee?" I was going for the tea since I wanted to sleep tonight. Coffee in the late afternoon was a big fat no unless I wanted to have a night out.

"English breakfast, please."

"Coming right up." As I got the cups out of the cupboard, I could feel his gaze on me. Well, I thought I could. It wasn't as if I was going to turn and check. I fumbled the cups as I put them on the counter, and they fell the last inch with loud clinks.

"Do you need some help?"

"Ah, no. I'm quite capable of breaking things all by myself." I chuckled, and so did he. As I made the tea, I ignored the warmth low in my belly. The heartbreak just wouldn't be worth it, and I had to work with him. Platonic friends all the way.

His chair scraped back. He stood and went to the fridge. "Mind if I get this famous cake out? I can't do nothing."

"Oh, okay. It's the only cake in there. You can't miss it." Why did he have to be so polite? If he was a bit ruder, more like Adam, it would be so easy to ignore his looks and the one-sided attraction I had going on.

He got the cake out and found my plates and spoons. By the time he'd set it up on the table, the tea was ready. "Milk and sugar?" I asked as I set the cups on the table.

"White and one, please." I grabbed the milk from the fridge and handed it to him. The sugar bowl was already on the table. Everyone liked their tea just so, and I didn't want to spoil it for him.

Once we'd sat and served ourselves, he took a giant whiff of the cake. "Mmm, this looks fantastic and smells delicious. How could you hold out on me like that?" He pinned me with his pretty eyes, and I couldn't help but wonder if he meant something else as well. *Ha ha, you wish. No, no I don't.*

I was such a bad liar, even with all my practice. "I told you; it was an accident. And on that note, we'd best save a piece for Carina. She'll spit chips if she knows we kept cake from her."

He laughed. "Agreed. I don't want your demise to become the next story the paper has to run."

"Ha ha." I sipped my tea. I didn't want to pry, but after seeing his sister today, my annoying curiosity won out. I sincerely hoped she was okay. "How was lunch with your sister? She seems nice, if a bit shy."

His gaze blanked, and the affable demeanour of a moment ago disappeared. He lowered his spoon to his plate. "She's okay. It was nice to see her. We don't get together enough."

Might as well make this as awkward as possible. Besides, he might want to talk about it. Some people just needed prodding. "Is everything okay?"

He stared at me, maybe weighing up whether he wanted to spill or not. "She's okay. Why are you asking?"

The little pang in my heart told me he was being a protective brother, and there was definitely more to this. I cared about what she was going through because I cared about him. Were we becoming better friends, or was it just me becoming too attached? If it was Carina and her sister, I'd definitely be asking the same questions, so I'd assume it was because we were friends. Why was it so hard for me to accept that I wasn't unlikable? Too many years around toxic people would do that, I supposed. "Can I be honest?"

He nodded. "Please, go ahead. I wouldn't want anything less."

"She didn't look well, and you seem... stressed by the whole thing. I mean, you don't have to tell me anything, but if you want to talk about it, I'm here. And I won't repeat any of it to anyone—not Meg, not Bailey, and not Carina. I promise. If you don't want to talk about it, that's okay too." There. That wasn't so hard now, was it? I could do this friend thing and show I cared, even if putting myself out there was difficult. If he shut me down, that was okay. This wasn't about me.

He ran a hand through his long fringe, sweeping it back before the strands slid back into place a little mussed. It wasn't sexy. Not. At. All. I slapped myself across the face. His eyes widened. "What did you just do?"

"I thought I felt a mosquito biting me. They love me. If there's one in a hundred-mile radius, it'll feed on me. Sorry. So, did you want to talk about it?"

He peered at me, maybe making sure I wasn't going to have another episode. "Okay, but please don't say anything to anyone. I don't like talking about my sister. Macpherson is the only one who knows some of it. When things got bad last year, I had to take a couple of weeks of unpaid leave."

I hoped my eyes conveyed how sincere I was and how much I cared. "Oh, wow, that's not good. I promise not to tell anyone, ever."

"My sister's always been what you would call spiritual. She went to church every week, even though my parents and I didn't. Not that I don't believe in God, but I'm on the fence. I like proof, and, well, no one's given me any yet, and, in fact, all the crap my sister's been through, where was God then?" He pressed his lips together for a moment, anger flashing through his gaze. "Anyway, a couple of years ago, she met a young woman there about her age. Sophia." He took a deep breath and looked past me for a moment, cake and tea forgotten. When he looked back at me, he'd composed himself. "She'd brought Sophia and a couple of the other girls back to my parents' one day, and apparently Sophia saw a photo of me and my sister. She started bugging my sister about meeting me. At the same time, she was getting closer to Hannah."

Obviously, Sophia was going to prove to be a problem, but how? I leaned forward, my own cake and tea forgotten. "So, what happened?"

"Over time, they became best friends, and Hannah introduced us." He sighed. "Sophia flirted, was cute, the usual. Anyway, she seemed fun, and I fell for her. We were together for seven months before everything fell apart." Regret clouded his expression. It soon turned to anger again.

"I'm sorry. Was it something specific?" The hurt on his face made me want to reach across the table and grab his hand, but I didn't. He had obviously come to terms with things—he was dating again, albeit not getting serious with anyone—and he seemed okay in general.

"She became clingy and bossy... with both of us. Had to know where I was all the time, used emotional blackmail, and cried when I wasn't available to talk when she wanted. But the last straw was with Hannah. She conned Hannah into the fact that she could see ghosts." He cradled his cup between large hands, then slowly turned it around and around. "Our grandmother had died just before Sophia came onto the scene, and she kept telling my sister that she had messages for us. We were close to my grandmother, and her death hit my sister hard. They were best friends. Anyway, she bought into the crap. When she finally found out Sophia was lying and using her for money, she tried to kill herself." His top lip kinked up in a sneer.

I swallowed. Out of all the things it could've been, this was it. There was no way in Hades I could ever admit to him that I could see ghosts. It would be the end of our friendship, which meant there would always be a wall between us. There was part of myself I could never admit to with him. And if you couldn't totally be yourself with someone, how good a relationship could you really have?

My stomach dropped, and it was all I could do not to slam my hand on it to stop the freefall. I took a deep breath. "Didn't your sister have any other friends? People she could trust and turn to?" I'll admit that I didn't see why that would push Hannah so far. Yes, everyone dealt with things differently, but she hadn't known Sophia that long.

"My sister struggled growing up. You might have noticed that she's shy. She was relentlessly teased at school and didn't have many friends. The couple she did have went to other cities for university, and they drifted away. When Hannah was accepted by the young church set, it really made her feel good, like she was popular. Unfortunately, it was all a sham. Sophia even tried to get money from me. She asked to borrow five thousand pounds because her mother was going to go be evicted for unpaid rent and bills. I checked it out, and turns out that her mother lives in a palatial flat in London and has plenty of money. I tried to talk to Hannah about it, but she didn't believe me. Until it was too late."

I bit my bottom lip. "What an evil POS. Did she get any money out of Hannah?"

His furious gaze met mine, his fists clenched on the table. "My sister had been saving for a flat. Every time Sophia wanted more money, she said she had news from my grandmother, but she wouldn't pass the message over until Hannah paid. She fleeced her out of twenty-two thousand pounds—ten thousand of those were from her inheritance from our grandmother. Thank God my dad found out at that stage and went to the police. That's when Sophia called my sister and told her off, said she was only friends with her because the pastor asked her to, and that my sister was a loser. She disappeared after that, and the police said there's nothing they can do about it because my sister gave her the money willingly."

My mouth dropped open. "Hades! That's disgusting. I'm so, so sorry." Watching all the emotions flay his face made me want to cry. I admit I couldn't totally relate since my sister and I weren't that close, but if someone had done that to her, I'd be furious, same if they did it to Carina or Meg. The fact this fly excrement had done it to Finnegan made me angry enough. "Your sister just looks sad and maybe like she's not eating well."

"She's not eating well. She's had anorexia before, survived it after suffering when she was fourteen and fifteen. This brought everything back, and she's relapsed. She's seeing a psychologist, and my parents are doing everything they can, but it breaks my heart. She was such a happy kid up until she was about eight or nine. Anyway, that's the story. Hannah means everything to me, and I blame myself in some ways. If I hadn't dated that pig's swill, perhaps she would've moved on and Hannah wouldn't have trusted her so much. I don't know." He put his elbows on the table and rested his face in his hands. A muffled "It was all my fault," came through.

That was it. I couldn't take it any more.

I went to the other side of the table and put a hand on his back. "It's not your fault. People like that prey on certain personalities. They know who to target. Your sister and you are both victims. It proves you're both nice because you assumed she was coming from a good place. Abusers use people's good characters against them. They know exactly what they're doing. And the more they know you, the more ammunition they have. They chip away at your self-esteem, they gaslight, they slowly push you so far down that you can't get a clear view of anything but what they choose to show you." I rubbed his back, hoping it reinforced my words. "It's clear you did what you could and then some. Please don't blame your-self." No wonder he didn't want to date seriously any more. He didn't trust himself. His sister wasn't the only one he was trying to protect. It took one to know one.

He relaxed under my touch. As he sat back, I removed my hand. When he looked up at me with his beautiful blue eyes, my breath caught. I'd never seen him so vulnerable or grateful. "Thanks, Avery. I appreciate it." The smile he gave me was sad.

"Any time. That's what friends are for." And if that's all we ever were, that was fine. Let's not talk about how that thought stabbed my heart in a way I didn't want. The pain was way better than getting even closer to him to only be rejected later. Better to be safe than sorry wasn't a cliché for nothing. I went back to my side of the table and sat. To hide whatever was going on in my heart, I lifted my cup to my face and took a long sip of tea.

Banging came from the front door, and I started. Finnegan looked at me. "Are you expecting anyone?"

"Ah, no. The buzzer didn't sound either." Had Mrs Crabby let someone in? What if it was Adam? Surely he couldn't come in unless invited. I glanced at my bag on the table. It would look weird if I grabbed my stone... *crystal* out of there. I reluctantly stood and went to the door.

"Avery, open up. I know you're in there." For an old lady, Mrs Crabby sure had a powerful angry voice.

What had I done now? I opened the door. "Hi, what's up?" I smiled and gave off an air of calm like she wasn't standing there, her face contorted in fury. She held up a plastic container the size of a lunchbox. My face scrunched. Three dead, bloodied rats without eyes sat in the container. What in Hades?

"What's the meaning of these?" She jiggled the container near my face, and my head jerked back, my chin jamming into my neck.

"I don't know. Dead rats. Where did you find them?" What was it with me and rats? Whenever someone wanted to upset me, dead rats turned up.

She narrowed her eyes and peered at me. "You didn't leave these on the front fence?"

"No, of course not. Why would I do that?"

She pressed her lips together. *Hmm, can't answer that, can you, Crabby?* "Well, who else would do it?"

"I have no idea. Have you made any enemies lately?" She probably had. Was she that oblivious to how awful she was?

"Of course not. What about you? Journalists are always making enemies. One of yours almost killed me. Don't think I'll ever forget it."

I shut my mouth lest my sigh escape. Like that was my fault. Besides, I did feel guilty about it. "Look, I'm sorry, but I don't think this has anything to do with me. I'll keep an eye out."

She leaned towards me and stuck her head in the door. Her face relaxed. "Hello, Finnegan. How are you?"

He stood and came to the door. "Good thanks, Mrs Collins. How have you been?"

"Oh, you know, getting by. My arthritis is always bothering me, and I still have occasional headaches after that man Avery knows attacked me." She threw a dirty look my way before smiling at Finnegan. Why did he get all the love? Looked like even Mrs Crabby wasn't immune to a good-looking man.

"If you need anything, let me know." He smiled.

"Thank you, Finnegan. If only everyone was so kind." I hadn't imagined the glance she flicked at me. Seriously? Argh. "Just be careful of this one. She's trouble." Wow, harsh. I didn't actually know what to say. Even though I expected the worst from her, it still came as a shock sometimes.

Finnegan put his arm around my shoulders and pulled me into his side. Even as I told myself not to, I melted into his side and hoped he couldn't hear my thunderous heartbeat. *Don't turn your head and nuzzle him. Don't do it, Avery. Focus on Crabby.* "Avery's a great friend. She's not trouble, far from it, in fact. She just believes in getting to the truth."

"Hmph. If you say so." She rubbed one hip. "I'm off. If either of you see anything, let me know."

"Will do." Finnegan answered for both of us. I was still dazed.

When she was halfway down the stairs, he took his arm away,

and I shut the door. I made sure my expression was neutral when I looked at him. "Thanks for that. She loves to give me a hard time." It was nice to have someone stick up for me. In my old life, it never happened.

He shook his head. "She's always been nice to me, but I've seen how she is with some people. Her bark's worse than her bite."

"Yeah, well, as long as she doesn't kick me out. Rentals this cheap are hard to come by, especially around here. I guess I have Daisy now, so I could always commute." That calmed me down. I had some savings now—not a lot, but more of a buffer than before. And because of Daisy, I could live fifteen or twenty minutes away. There were places that had more rentals than Manesbury, so at least I wouldn't be out in the street if she decided to throw me out on a whim.

His forehead wrinkled. "Why would she throw you out? It's not like you have loud parties."

"She's threatened it a few times." I shrugged.

"Well, if she does, let me know. You can rent one of my bedrooms. I've got three, so there's plenty to go around." He smiled.

Oh, Hades, no. What a disaster that would be. "Um… thank you. That's super kind, but hopefully I won't need to. I try and stay out of her way, but whenever something goes wrong, I'm the first person she comes to see. Besides, it was my fault she was attacked. She has got a small point."

"It wasn't your fault… well, not directly. You don't get a say in what crazy people do, and you need to do your job."

"Thanks. Anyway, the cake is getting lonely and wondering why we haven't eaten it." I grinned.

Finnegan's dimple appeared as his lips curled up in a wide smile. "What are we waiting for?"

"What are we waiting for, indeed?" As we ate our delicious late-afternoon tea, my mind circled back to the rats. The only *person* I thought could be responsible made the blood freeze in my veins because he wasn't a person any more.

Adam.

If he'd become a poltergeist, I was in a giant manure mound of trouble.

That night, I slept with my banishing crystal gripped tightly in my hand. A fog of nightmares blackened my dreams, but even they couldn't stop me from wanting the night to last forever. Because when morning came, I'd have to face an angry spirit, and so much could go wrong. What in Hades was I going to do?

CHAPTER 14

Saturday morning I slept in—I didn't have to go to the rugby club until later, and after waking several times from nightmares, I needed the rest. Plus, I was in no hurry to go outside. When I finally managed to get up, I looked out the window. The fence was bare, thank Hades. After guzzling my coffee, I reluctantly called Celeste. If anyone could help me with Adam, it was her. Two of us banishing him had to be better than one, right?

"I'm sorry, Avery, but I can't get there today. Are you sure he's the one who left the rats?"

"No, not 100 per cent. But what if it was?"

The silence on the other end of the phone went for a beat too long. "You should be okay. Killing a rat is much easier than killing a person, and what's not to say he found them dead and just put them there?" Her hesitant voice wasn't reassuring in the least.

"Also, I can't stand out the front and battle a spirit. My landlady is looking for any excuse to kick me out. She already thinks I'm crazy." Maybe I could sneak out the back and walk around the long, long, long way to my car. I could walk parallel to the fences until I came to a laneway that led into the village. It would mean doing a whole loop of the village I didn't need to, but I had plenty of time.

"If you quietly repeat the words I told you, it will still work. The banishment doesn't require shouting. It makes no difference. And yes, two of us are stronger than one, but you've got this. If he did kill the rats and put them there, he's probably weakened. He'll need rest. He might not even be there this morning. In fact, after he's expended so much energy is the time to banish him. Let me know how you get on. I'm sorry, but I have to go now. Text me later. Bye, Avery."

"Ah, yeah, bye." I hung up. I should know better than to think someone I hardly knew would come all this way to help. Of course she had a life, and I was being a nuisance. I shouldn't have bothered her. Well, next time, I'd deal with it myself. There must be more I could learn from the net. But how to know what to believe and what not to. There'd be heaps of false information out there, like there was on any topic. Problem was, if I needed a new skill and didn't get it right, there would be consequences. I sighed.

My phone rang. Bellamy's name flashed on the screen. "Hello, Sergeant. How are you?"

"Sorry to bother you on a Saturday, but how's the investigation going?"

"I'm going back to the rugby club this arvo, when they have training. I have a few suspects, but there might be more. I also wanted to see if I could narrow it down before we caught up."

"Can you come in and see me when you're done? The mayor is breathing down my neck." Someone called out in the background. "I'll see you later, Winters." The call ended.

I chuckled. It wasn't a request—it was an order. What did I care? He was paying me, after all. The extra money I'd made from this would all be savings. I hadn't had time to stop and reflect on that with everything that had been going on, but once I had enough of an emergency buffer, I could consider saving up for specific things like a trip to Paris. A kernel of excitement settled in my belly. Since I'd arrived, I hadn't had the time or brain space to think about seeing some of Europe and more of the UK, but it was possible. My life had changed so much in the last six months. Who would've thought I was going to have these incredible opportunities? Dealing with cranky ghosts was a price I was willing to pay.

Instead of sitting around stressing about whether Adam would be waiting for me later, I stretched, practiced some hapkido, carried out more research into Ms Oatlands and her deceased husband, plus I cyberstalked Adam's girlfriend and her friend Peta. I figured they wouldn't be at the club since it was Saturday, and I might need to get more info another way.

Scrolling the girlfriend's Instagram had my eyebrows shooting up. I leaned forward and stared at the picture. A picture of Cath smiling next to a target in a field, her thumbs up in a gesture of triumph. The handle of the knife protruding from the bullseye shone silver in the bright daylight. Could it be that easy to solve this? He was killed with a knife to the back. But if she had killed him, would she have left this picture up? A quick look at her profile revealed a handful of other knife-throwing shots over the last year and a half and one video. She was scarily accurate. Note to self: don't annoy her too much. If it was her, I'd have to find out what set her off. Had she known about his affairs all along and had just played dumb, biding her time?

As I pondered the new information, my phone alarm went off—it was time to call Charles and Sergeant Fox.

They appeared simultaneously in front of the couch where I stood. Sergeant Fox gave me a nod. "Afternoon, Miss Winters."

"Hello, Sergeant Fox. Great to see you again. How have you been?"

His head tilted to the side. "Good, thank you. Charles has been helping me a great deal, putting to bed some of my ghosts, so to speak." He gave Charles a proud smile.

Charles blushed. Who knew ghosts could do that? "Thanks, Sergeant. I love helping." Charles finally looked at me. "Hey, Avery."

"Hey, Charles. Thanks for helping me with this."

Sergeant Fox raised his brows. "Yes, but you're helping me too. Sergeant Bellamy is a credit to the force, and Manesbury and its surrounds would be much safer if he stays where he is. I'm not

DIONNE LISTER

pleased at the likes of the mayor threatening him, especially when his nephew is hardly a pillar of society. Charles has told me your experiences and research into the matter. The sooner we put this to bed, the better."

Charles's eyes widened. "Oh, I forgot to tell you. A ghost called Earl Oatlands contacted me in the other realm. He asked for your help. Word's really getting around about you, Avery."

"Oh, wow, okay. I've actually been wanting to talk to him. I interviewed his wife the other day about candles."

"Yeah, he told me. She killed him, and she did some wicca stuff, and he's trapped in the backyard. He only managed to get a message to me for you because the previous owner of the house who died a long time ago can visit him, and after you saw him, he figured there might be a way to get in touch with you. He can't move on until he's freed, and he's miserable. If his wife dies and he's still trapped, he'll be stuck for eternity."

My mouth dropped open. "That's horrific." Ms Oatlands was evil. What was wrong with people? Also, who made her God? How did she think she had the right to decide whether someone should suffer for eternity or not? "Of course I'll help."

"Okay, thanks. He needs you to make her free him. I've got some information that I'll give you later since we've got work to do now. She's a massive scammer, apparently."

"Interesting. Thanks for passing that on. If you see Earl again, tell him I'm only too happy to help, but I'm not sure when. I'll have to come up with a plan, and I'm kind of in the middle of Adam's case at the moment." It wouldn't be as easy as marching in there and demanding she free him. There would need to be incentive, and I didn't know what yet.

Fox cleared his throat. "Time's ticking, Miss Winters."

"It is. I guess we should go. The only thing is… Adam might be waiting for me outside, and I don't know how stable he is. He might have turned into a poltergeist."

Both ghosts widened their eyes. "That's not good news, Miss Winters."

"Indeed, Sergeant, it's not. Our advantage is that I have a

banishing stone, but also, if we explain that we're trying to solve his murder, it should placate him." I wasn't going to mention that he was angry last night because of Finnegan, or was it because I was ignoring him? I crossed my fingers that solving his crime would mean he went to hell ASAP. Not that I would wish that on many people, but Adam was dangerous and horrible. If anyone deserved to be there, it was him. He could hang out with Charles's father.

Charles took a step closer to Fox, then looked at me. "Are you sure Adam won't try and hurt us?"

"I'm not positive, but you guys can disappear if anything happens. He can't do much to me." How strong was he? Surely not strong enough to possess me. Wouldn't that be the poo icing on the vomit cake of my life—being controlled by a misogynistic ghost. I huffed a laugh to myself. "About the worst of it is probably him throwing a few stones or something. Besides, I have my banishing crystal. The only issue with it is Mrs Crabby seeing me and making a big deal about how crazy I am." Even though I was dealing with ghosts, things still had real-world consequences.

Sergeant Fox gave a nod, his expression no-nonsense. He was ready for action, a policeman through and through. "So, are we all good to head out?"

"Yep." I slung my bag over my shoulder and held the crystal firmly in one hand. As I descended the stairs, I repeated the banishing incantation in my head. Sucking in a deep breath, I opened the door.

It was time to battle.

Adam stood on the other side of the fence, his arms folded. He smirked. "Did you like my little present?"

I put my phone to my ear and made sure my voice didn't waver. "What present?" There was no way I was going to let him get to me. My vow to stand up to the rubbish humans in my life extended to ghosts.

His eyes narrowed. "You're lying."

I made my gait as relaxed as possible and the expression on my face clueless. "Nope, not lying. I have no idea what you're talking about."

There was no point having him around, so I stepped out of the front gate and stopped next to him. Facing the street—because I didn't want Mrs Crabby to see my face—I whispered the incantation. My heart raced. This was totally going to cheese him off, and there was a risk he'd try and hurt me when he came back, but hopefully this would slow the rate of his gathering strength.

Adam, for all his outdated ideas on being a male, wasn't totally stupid. "Don't you banish me again. Do it and—" He popped out of existence, and I let my breath whoosh out. That wasn't so hard after all. Crystals for the win. Never thought I'd be saying that.

"Nicely done, Miss Winters."

"Thank you, Sergeant."

Charles stood next to me and reached to hold my hand. A chill engulfed my palm as his hand passed through. He stared at his hand, then shook his head slowly before looking up at me. "I'm glad you're okay. That ghost scared me. I don't want him to hurt you."

The urge to hug him overwhelmed me. This loyal, sweet boy whose life was cut short in the cruellest of ways. If I ever had kids, I could only hope they'd be as kind as Charles. I tried to put my hand on his shoulder, but it fell through the coldness. I sighed. "Thanks. And thanks for being here for me." I looked from Charles to Sergeant Fox. "Both of you."

The sergeant cleared his throat and gave an awkward nod before walking towards my car. "We don't want to be late."

Charles and I shared a smile. Sergeant Fox might not be comfortable showing his soft side, but we both knew he had one.

As I hopped in the car, my phone dinged with a message. Meg. I smiled. It was a group message. *Hey, Aves, Carina, dinner tonight? I've got the night off. Thought we might hit up a great steak place in Cranstonbury. You ladies in?*

I texted back. *Defo. What time? Who's driving?*

I'll pick you up at seven.

Carina's message came through, and she was coming. Yay for dinner out. I could do with a fun night. This Adam business was wearing me down.

Fox and Charles were both quiet on the way there, as was I. I was hoping that just my presence at the training would shake some information loose. The parking lot was three-quarters full—a good sign. The more people here, the better. I parked and turned to Sergeant Fox who was in the front passenger seat. "If you and Charles can listen in to different people, that would be great. If seeing me doesn't start them talking about Adam, move to the next person. We need to cover as many people as possible. I know that's a big ask. Sorry. We really need an army of ghosts."

Charles leaned over and stuck his head in between the seats. "Why don't you call Ev?"

"Good idea. I didn't think of that. Come to think of it, are there any other ghosts we can call as well?" Everly might be busy, but I could try.

"How many do you need?" Fox asked.

I had a quick think. "Could we get another ten? That should cover it."

"On it." Sergeant Fox popped away.

I looked at Charles. "Why couldn't he just call them?"

"They might not hear. He's probably gone to one of the other realms to see who's there. Why don't you call Ev?"

"Okay." I called out, and after a minute of Charles and me staring around the car waiting, she popped into the back seat next to Charles.

"Avery, what's going on? I was in the middle of counselling someone."

"Oh, sorry. I was hoping you could help me for fifteen minutes or so, but if not, that's okay." The work she did was important, and guilt slid over me. I hated being a bother.

Charles wasn't so worried, apparently. "Avery needs our help solving a crime. It's important. Sergeant Bellamy's job is on the line if we don't find out who killed someone quickly. Can you please stay?"

Her expression relaxed, and she smiled. "Of course I can help. Justine can wait for me. I'll just let her know. Be back in a jiffy." She disappeared. Less than a minute later, she reappeared. "Sorted. Now what?"

I explained what we were doing, and once that explanation was done, Fox arrived in the car with ten other ghosts. So now we had thirteen. Wasn't that unlucky? Hopefully not.

I shrunk back against my door as chills assaulted me. The car was jam-packed with spirits. They overlapped each other and me. This was not ideal. My brain found it hard to cope, my amygdala screaming at me to get out and run. The freezer-like atmosphere wasn't helping because I couldn't stop shivering.

"I've explained what I want of everyone." Fox's voice floated to me from behind a wall of other spirits. I couldn't see him.

"I'm getting out now. Can I get a couple of spirits to go inside the clubhouse too? If they can find others there, I'd like them to listen in, especially if there are any young women in there."

"Understood." Fox called out two names and put them on that detail.

My racing heart thudded loudly in my ears, and I couldn't stay put any longer. I reached through the creepy crowd to where I knew my bag was on the front seat and grabbed it. To say I jumped out of the car was an understatement. I pressed the button on my fob to lock it and stood there rubbing my arms. That was freaky, and I never wanted to experience that again. After one last shudder, I made my way to the rugby field.

Like before, the players were on the field running drills. They ran in a line down the field, passing the ball one to the other. The sleazy assistant coach stood on the sideline watching. Hmm, a quick survey of the area revealed the head coach wasn't there. I pulled up a photo of him on my phone and showed it to Charles who had stayed with me from my walk from the car. "See this guy," I said quietly out of the side of my mouth. "Can you go inside and see if you can find him? If you do find him, hang out to see what he's up to, then come let me know. Obviously, if you can't find him, let me know as soon as you can. If you find others in there, maybe check them out before coming back."

"Will do." He ran across the grass to the clubhouse. Luckily, it was a public building and not a private home. Charles reached the door, then disappeared inside. The other ghosts positioned themselves around the field, and one of them also went inside the club-house. If I wanted this to work, I'd have to make it clear I was here to ask more questions. Three players and the young man who ran errands were on the sideline near the assistant coach—one of the players was the one who refused to talk to me the other day. I steeled myself and went over. There was a chance I'd get kicked out, but if that happened, I'd make as much of a scene as I could. The whole exercise was about getting people talking to each other. Not that I'd complain if someone decided to give me more information directly.

My voice was loud enough to carry to some of the players on the field as I addressed their comrades on the sideline. "Hey, I was wondering if I could speak to you about Adam. The police are still trying to figure out who killed him, and I was hoping to get some more information for my article. I heard via the grapevine that he wasn't as loved as the club and previous media reports said."

The tallest of them stepped towards me, his brow furrowed and eyes narrowed. He swore at me. "Get out of here. That's a load of bull. We all loved Adam." As he stepped into my personal space, despite the rush of adrenaline through my body, I stood my ground. He wouldn't hit or push me here in front of all these people, would he?

"What are you doing here, Miss Winters?" The assistant coach moved to stand in front of me, next to the thug. "You'd better leave. You're not welcome here." Hmm, he'd changed his tune. Apparently, he didn't want to date me any more. *Oh, what a shame.*

Some of the players hurried over, maybe curious as to what was happening. The guy who'd said not two words to me the other day continued his silence, but he gave me the subtlest of nods. Ah, interesting. Before they could kick me out, I reached into my bag and pulled out business cards. I handed them out. "If anyone has anything they want to say, call me. You can do it anonymously."

Byron, the errand boy—not that he was a boy, but errand young man sounded weird—gave panicked looks around at the team members, his gaze stopping on one in particular. I made a mental note of what he looked like—around five foot eleven, curly red hair, beard, blue eyes, freckles. Was Byron worried about what might come out? Did the young man know something? How did this other guy figure into things?

The assistant coach moved faster than I thought his chubby body could go as he swiped my cards out of players' hands.

"I work for the *Manesbury Daily*. You can also call or email our office. I'm Avery Winters."

The mood shifted. The men stopped staring at me and looked behind me. I turned. The head coach was finally coming. A man in a business suit was walking from the clubhouse to the parking lot. Hmm, a meeting? What that was about? Might be nothing, but might not be.

The coach looked at his players. "Get back to training. Now!" They immediately jogged off. I didn't miss the dirty looks three of his players gave him—the quiet nodder, a tall guy with brown hair and a beard, and the guy who'd said a few things to me the other day, quiet nodder's friend. Those were the three I'd need to target afterwards. When everyone was back on the field, the coach turned to me. "I don't know why you're back, but you need to leave. We're not saying anything else about Adam."

"I would've thought you'd want the police to solve this case. Do you have something to hide?" It was nice to be able to say exactly what I was thinking. "Everyone goes on about how nice Adam was, what a hero, but he's a cheater and a misogynist, isn't he? Or do you all respect that here? Are women no more than trash to you and your club?"

Byron's eyes widened. Looked like someone was still paying attention. The guy who'd tried to intimidate me before stuck his middle finger up at me. Mmm, charming. Such a catch. Probably Adam's best friend.

The coach looked at Byron. "Please escort this woman off the grounds." He looked at me. "I'll be applying for a restraining order. We don't want to see you around here again."

"Yes, because I'm so threatening. Me, a small woman against a team of massive rugby players. The truth will come out, whether you want it to or not. You're looking mighty suspicious right now."

Anger flickered in his eyes. His jaw muscles bunched, but instead of taking my bait, he jerked around and folded his arms, his gaze on the field.

"Please don't make this any harder than it has to be." Byron looked at me apologetically. "Come on."

Was I a journalist? Yes. Was I going to talk as we walked? Of course. "Did you like Adam?"

Byron gave me the side eye. "Yes, of course." His tone was flat— whether that was because he didn't like him, or he was being wary was another thing.

"What was so good about him?"

"He was the best player at the club. He was... ah... good at getting the guys motivated."

"Did anyone dislike him?" I watched his face carefully. He kept looking forward. It was impossible to miss that his lips pressed together, as if he was willing them not to open. "Well? You know I'm not the enemy here. I just want to get to the truth."

We'd reached the open gate leading to the car park. Charles had exited the building and was making his way towards me, a smile on his face. What I would give for some good news.

"Here we are, Miss Winters." He stopped and gestured for me to keep walking. "I hope you get to the bottom of it." Funny how I didn't believe him. He wasn't quite convincing. He turned and walked away.

"I know you're all hiding something. I'll find out what it is." Was that more for me? Who knew? But it did mean they were on alert now. Maybe trying to cover something up now I'd given them the proverbial kick up the backside would bring them undone. Unless they'd already covered everything up. Would it be too much to ask that the ghosts had some information?

I went to my car, and after checking no spirits lurked inside, I unlocked it and hopped in. Charles seeped through the passenger door and sat in the front seat.

"So gross."

He stared at me, forehead wrinkled. "What?"

"You leaking through the door. It's gross. Can you just pop into existence next time?"

He rolled his eyes. "Seriously? If I pop, you complain I surprised you. Now you're saying I can't *leak*. Man, I can't win. What's a ghost to do? You alive people are such a pain." He sighed dramatically.

I grinned. "Yep, we are. So what did you find out?"

"Should we wait until Fox is here? That way, we can all know everything."

That moment when a child was smarter than you. Okay, so the *child* was way older than me, but still…. "Good idea. He and the other ghosts are probably still listening in on stuff." When you dropped a bomb, the fallout lasted more than one minute.

While we waited, I got out my notebook and wrote all the things I wanted to remember about today, including peoples' reactions to what I'd said. I'd be seeing Bellamy straight after this, and I wanted him to have all the information. Even though I formed opinions on things, he would have his own way of assessing it all as a policeman with years and years of experience. He would likely see a lot more than me and could give me a direction to go in rather than chasing up every person and piece of information, which was what the journalist in me wanted to do.

Finally, Fox popped into the car, right on top of Charles. "Get in the back seat."

"Yes, sir." Charles floated out of the back of the passenger seat. Argh, not again.

I looked at Fox. "Did anyone say anything interesting?"

"I met with all my comrades, and I have much to report. Is your pen ready?"

I held it up. "Ready and waiting." When he was done, Charles told us what he overheard and saw. I didn't know whether to be happy or sad. They'd overheard so much that I would be running around for weeks investigating everyone, and there was only so much I could tell Bellamy. There was no way he'd believe some people had admitted that much out in the open, and how much time had I been here? Not to mention that if he ever asked anyone to verify what I'd "heard," they wouldn't because they hadn't actually said it to me.

My phone dinged with a text from Bellamy. *When can I expect to see you? Are you finished at the rugby club?*

Finished at the club and maybe finished for good. How much of these many pages of notes could I disclose? That was the question. I had to see him in less than thirty minutes, and I still didn't have an answer.

I'd better hurry up and figure it out.

CHAPTER 15

I sat in Bellamy's office, across the table from where he sat clicking his stapler. The department must go through a lot of staples. Fox stood in his normal place behind Bellamy's chair, and Charles sat in the chair next to me. It was nice to have them here. If I went off track, they could remind me of what to say or add anything they'd forgotten to tell me. It was also Fox's job to shake his head if I went too far. We'd roughly agreed on what I should disclose and what I should leave out, but it didn't hurt to have the prompts, just in case.

I looked at item one on my list. "So, I have his partner, Cath, as the first name on the list. She's competent with knives, and he was cheating on her."

"We knew about the knives but not the cheating. She didn't say anything when my officers interviewed her. Did she know?"

"I overheard her telling someone else that she'd known for a week before his death. It seems as if she recently found out, but maybe she knew months ago and was acting so no one thought it could possibly be her? Also, when I saw her the other day, she had a black eye. Claimed it was from walking into a door after crying so much." I likely didn't need to state the obvious, that maybe Adam had hit her when she attacked him. He might have elbowed her after she stabbed him and never saw her since he claimed he didn't know who killed him. I also doubted he'd send me on a wild goose chase if he knew who the murderer was.

His brow furrowed at that last bit. "Hmm." He typed the information into his desktop computer, the monitor sitting slightly off to the side so he could look at me when we were talking. "Okay. Next."

"There are two gay men on the team, and from what people were saying, Adam used to give them a hard time about it. There was always some snide comment. I looked up their social media, and sure enough, there are rude comments on posts that are about being gay. When challenged, Adam always says 'It was just a joke.'" Hmm, he'd said that to me too about a particularly sexual comment. His jokes weren't funny, but were they enough to get him killed? I hated that we had to look into people who had been victimised, but Bellamy's job was on the line, and that came first.

He leaned back in his chair and thankfully left the stapler on the desk. "Something to investigate, but I don't know that we can call that a motive for murder. Did he do anything else to them, like play pranks, be rougher than normal?"

I casually glanced at Fox, and he shrugged. I looked back at Bellamy. "Not that I know of, but I didn't get to ask. Something to chase up?"

He rubbed his chin in thought. After a bit, he said, "Not at this stage. Give me the men's names, and I'll have one of my guys look into their pasts. If they've had no violent incidents, I think they're not on the top of our list."

"Okay." I made a note next to their names. Didn't mean I wouldn't try and get more about it, but as far as Bellamy was concerned, that was it. "Right, the next one is something I overheard. I wasn't told this directly." Okay, so a ghost told me, but this was how I was playing it. It was too important to not tell him.

Bellamy leaned forward and placed his forearms on the table, linking his hands. "Do go on."

"This afternoon, Coach Atherton wasn't on the sidelines as per usual, so I snuck into the clubhouse."

"Why did you sneak?"

"He told me to leave the first time I was there. He doesn't want me nosing around, and I knew he wouldn't talk."

Bellamy nodded. "Hmm...." He typed something into his computer.

"So, anyway, I snuck in and heard him talking to someone in the men's change rooms. He said, 'If this gets out, the club will never recover.' Whoever was talking to him said, 'Looks like Adam's death came at the right time.' That's all I got. After hearing that, I wasn't going to hang around and be found out." What the secret was, we still had no idea, but those were some pretty incriminating words. They were also hearsay as far as the police were concerned, but it didn't mean Bellamy couldn't cast a microscope over the coach.

"Do you know who the other person was?"

I remembered the man leaving the clubhouse. "I saw him leaving a bit after I snuck out. He came out with the coach. About six foot, slim build, head shaved, maybe in his forties?" I couldn't tell him he had a scar above his top lip on his right side and that his eyes were brown since I'd only seen him from a distance. Fox's description meant I could look him up later. He and Charles were going to come over after this and help me while I googled everything.

Bellamy leaned forward and carefully typed the information into his computer... using two fingers. Watching him do that on a long-term basis would drive me nuts. Sooooo slow. He finally looked up. "What else did you discover?"

"No one said this to me directly, but I heard a couple of the players complaining that even though he was dead, he was still disrupting training and could this all go away. A guy called Dave also said he was a rubbish human who deserved what happened to him. He said that to one of the gay players I told you about before. About two-thirds of the team thought the sun shone out of his behind though, so the complainers were doing it quietly. The coach threw me out after that." I couldn't elaborate that David had the hots for Cath, Adam's partner. I didn't know how I could explain that. Did he help her kill him? Or did he do it by himself? What was the rest of the story there? I had so much work to do.

He sloth typed it out, then sat back. "Is that all?"

"Unfortunately, yes." Sheesh, I'd thought it was a lot. "I plan on researching more when I leave here. I'm going to check everyone's social media in more depth. If I can discover where some of these people go to have fun, I might be able to *accidentally* run into them. It would be even better if they were full of alcohol." I didn't tell him that one of the ghosts had overheard two of the players talking about the team going to Vibe tonight, a nightclub in Exeter. Maybe the girls would help me out after dinner. Hmm… that wasn't a bad idea. It would be the perfect opportunity. Alcohol tended to loosen people's tongues.

His forehead wrinkled. "Don't go putting yourself in danger. If you find out anything of note, call me straight away. You have my mobile. No matter what time of day or night. Understood?"

"I won't, as in, I won't put myself in danger. I promise to call as soon as I get anything you can act on."

He narrowed his eyes. "After last time, I don't know if I can trust that you won't risk yourself."

"I'm promising. If I think I'm talking to the killer, I'll call you straight away, and I won't go anywhere with them alone. I'll make sure the conversation is in a public place."

He gave me another look, confirming he didn't believe me. But I meant what I said. If he didn't trust me, that was his problem. "Hmph. I wouldn't have asked for your help if this wasn't such a difficult circumstance." He rubbed his forehead. "Mayor Murphy calls me every day, multiple times. Apparently, if I don't figure this out soon, not only will I be demoted, I'll be moved to a smaller station two hours from here."

What kind of monster was this mayor? "Yikes. That's horrible. I'll do what I can as quickly as I can… without putting myself in danger." I gave him a gentle smile.

He gave a half smile in return. "Don't forget to charge us for all of your time."

"I won't." I stood. "I guess that's it. I'll call you as soon as I have something else."

He stood and held out his hand for me to shake. "I appreciate it. Thank you. The sooner the better."

"I know, which is why I'm going to get started tonight. I have dinner with the girls. I'll see if they want to go clubbing afterwards."

He pressed his lips together, as if he was trying not to tell me to be careful again. He finally said, "Okay. Speak to you soon."

From behind Bellamy's chair, Fox said, "Thank you."

An icy chill seized my hand. It was Charles, trying to tug it. "We'll see you at your place." I gave the subtlest nod, and the ghosts disappeared.

Now I had some sleuthing to do. Hopefully it wasn't too much to ask to figure this out tonight—not only would I be saving Bellamy's skin, but I'd be getting Adam off my back too. With a bit of luck, solving this murder would see him leaving this realm for good. It was time to make it happen.

CHAPTER 16

Carina, Meg, and I stood in line outside Vibe nightclub, downwind of some serious cologne. I was onto my fourth sneeze. Being the awesome friends they were—how did that happen to me?—Meg and Carina had been keen to come out and help me fact find. It also helped that I drove and they could have a few drinks. Charles and Fox had asked if I wanted them to come and listen in, but this time, I needed to do this myself so I had no worries about passing on all the information to Bellamy.

An overeager woman in line behind me danced to the beat pulsing from inside the club and bumped my back, throwing me into Meg. She caught me.

I stepped back and apologised to Meg. Afterwards, I turned and gave the woman behind me a dirty look. She didn't even notice. Oh, the joy. I looked at my phone. "Seriously. It's almost eleven. We've been standing in line for almost twenty minutes." I wasn't generally an impatient person, but I hated time wasting, and this was total time wasting. If I didn't have people to spy on, I'd be much more relaxed about it. Who knew, I might even be enjoying hanging out with the girls. Maybe I should stop worrying about what I was doing here and have a bit of fun? The woman behind me slammed into me again. Fun? What was I thinking? I spun around, ignoring the skittering flutters in my stomach. Confrontation wasn't my favourite thing. "Excuse me, do you mind not bumping me? I'd really appreciate it."

Her and her similarly scantily dressed friend put their hands on their hips. The offending line dancer cocked her head to one side and looked me up and down. Yes, I was wearing three-quarter-length jeans and not a super-short skirt. So sue me. "I'm just having fun, old biddy. You should try it sometime."

I didn't react. Sure, she was probably eighteen, but how did twenty-six become an "old biddy?" Plus, I was often mistaken for being way younger when I was working. I couldn't win. Story of my life. "I'd be having a lot more fun if people weren't knocking into me every five seconds. Look, I don't want any trouble. Can you just be a bit more careful?" The last thing I needed was to get into a fight with a random woman and end up in a cell. Bellamy would not appreciate that one iota.

She smirked. I had absolutely no confidence in whatever she was about to say. "Yeah, sure."

"Thanks." My response didn't include a smile, but I had to at least pretend she was telling the truth. I turned back around.

Meg's eyes were wide. She kept her voice low as she leaned close to me. "Ooh, you told her. What's with her calling you old though? You look about twenty."

"I have no idea. And I don't care. I just want to get into this place."

A group of beefy, athletic-looking guys strolled up to the bouncer. They had a couple of gorgeous young women with them. Their tight-fitting, cut-out dresses revealed the lack of fat on their taut bodies. Lucky them. But then again, I didn't dislike my body. I was fit, but I drew the line at going hungry all the time. If I wanted a lemon tart, by God, I was going to have one. Food didn't let me down, that was people, so why should I ditch the stuff that brought me happiness?

As the guy who appeared to be the leader of this pack of privilege chatted to the bouncer, it hit me: it was Adam's rugby team. Of course, it took but a minute, and they were let straight in. No line waiting for them. I rolled my eyes.

Carina chuckled. "Ooh, dat's d'em, isn't it?"

I smiled. "How'd you guess?"

"I recognised one of d'em. D'e brunette d'at talked to the bouncer used to date a friend of mine. Lasted a couple of mont's."

"Oh, interest— Oof!" That idiot behind me had pushed me again, this time harder than before, and I flew into my friends, stomping on Meg's foot. Possum poo.

"Ouch!" Meg winced.

"I'm sorry, Meg. Are you all right?"

Before she could answer, a sarcastic voice came from over my shoulder. "Oh, my. I'm soooo sorry. Are you okay?"

I recovered and turned around. The girl had a mock-innocent expression on her face, her friend grinning like the cat who ate the canary. I had news for them—I wasn't a canary, and New Avery was someone who didn't take crap. Putting a hint of satisfaction into my smile, I stepped towards them. "Yes, thanks. I'm fine. Let me give you a hug to show there's no hard feelings." Before she knew what happened, I stepped into her and threw my arms around her waist, then grabbed the sensitive skin on her lower back and pinched and twisted. A nice little trick I learned in hapkido.

She yelped and jumped out of my embrace. Her mouth dropped open.

I grinned and leaned close to her face. My voice was low and creepy. "The dead talk to me. They tell me what to do." I straightened and grinned... a bit too much. Just the right amount of cray cray. "Have a great night." It was all I could do not to laugh. By the horrified look on her face, she thought I was as mad as a cut snake. Just the way I wanted it.

When I turned back to my ladies, Carina chuckled. "I don't know what you did or said to her, but it certainly made an impact." My pinch was subtle and quick. Hopefully no one noticed, which was how it was meant to be. Using hapkido in the wild was fun.

"I'm a journalist. I have a way with words." I gave her a cheesy smile.

"Thanks, Aves. I love it when you go all badass on people." Meg grinned; then something stole her attention. "Ooh, look, the line's moving." She bounced up and down excitedly. True to her observation, we moved forward. In the five more minutes it took us to get inside, I didn't feel so much as a breath of air from behind me. Who said violence never solved anything?

As expected, the inside of the club was dark and loud, beams of coloured light pulsing around the room. We pushed through the noisy throng to the bar where we joined yet another line. The dance floor was to our right and already crowded, the DJ playing up-tempo beats. To our left was a stairway that said "Get your eighties upstairs." So, two dance floors. This place must rake it in if both levels were as busy as each other. The vibe was good though. Everyone seemed to be having a great time.

After we got our drinks, I led the girls to a stand-up table so we could discuss tactics. I was having one vodka and orange, and I'd mainly hold it to look like I was having a few bevvies because someone might get sus if I wasn't drinking. As far as my quarries were concerned, I was off the clock.

I put my drink on a coaster and surveyed the room. "Right, so we need to find where the team are. It shouldn't be too hard to find a group of huge guys amongst this lot."

"You would think so, but there's a VIP area." Meg nodded to a mezzanine area that overlooked the dance floor. "The stairs are roped off, and there's a bouncer manning access."

"Ah, poo on a cracker. Is there a bar up there, or do they have to come down here for a drink?" I was pretty sure I was asking a stupid question, but a girl could hope.

"Sorry, love, but d'ey have d'eir own bar." Carina delivered the news in a kind voice. "But I'm sure we could get access if we tried."

My sigh was lost in the blaring music. "After getting kicked out of their home ground twice, they've probably handed my picture to the bouncers and told them to make sure I get nowhere near them." I was only half joking.

"Ah, but one of d'em dated my friend, remember? We got along well, me and Dave. D'eir break-up was mutual too. He's not a bad sort of fellow." She looked at my pretty, sleeveless pink shirt. "You could do wit' a bit of a wardrobe alteration. Live a little." She put her drink on the table, and undid an extra button, revealing most of my cleavage. "D'ere you go, you sexy little minx."

I looked down. I wasn't a prude, but it was more breast than I was used to showing. Not that I didn't want to be sexy, but I preferred when I first met a guy to know that he was out for more than a one-night stand. Once I confirmed he was a decent person, then I was happy to be as sexy as the next woman. But going full cleavage straight away was sending the wrong vibes.

Meg laughed. "You look gorgeous, Avery. Just go with it. Have a little fun." She winked.

Was I too uptight? Hmm, maybe. Maybe I just felt too vulnerable with my boobs out there for everyone to stare at, especially since my parents and Brad always told me I was nothing special— who the hell did I think I was? And their words had worked. I felt like an attention-seeking idiot. Surely everyone would see my boobs and think I was silly rather than sexy. I wasn't sexy. My habit of dressing plainly was probably also because I was rarely taken seriously as a journalist with my blonde, pretty-young-thing looks as it was. Getting the girls out would just make it worse. Why did I care so much though? Maybe it would make people underestimate me even more? Were there courses you could take to teach you how to use feminine attributes to your advantage? Hmm, I made a mental note to look it up. Who knew, maybe I could be sexy if I wanted?

Argh, stop overthinking! I needed to get out of my own head more often. Time for a sip of my drink as a distraction and maybe as a fortifying agent. Not that I was going to get drunk tonight. I needed my wits about me to remember what people said, and I was the designated driver. At least my memory for facts was good. It was an essential skill when reporting because you couldn't always record everything.

Carina looked past my shoulders towards the entrance. "Oh, dere's Bailey and Finny."

I spun around. Yep, two tall, hot guys dressed in button-up shirts and jeans walked towards us. *Grrr, body, now is not the time for tummy tingles*. If only I could turn off my libido whenever I wanted. I sighed, turned back to Meg, and yelled over the music, "What? What are they doing here?" I did not need any distractions.

Meg bopped away as she spoke. "I texted them when we were eating. Thought we could use back up. You know, just in case everything went pear-shaped like last time." I didn't see how things could go wrong in a packed club, as long as we didn't let anyone spike our drinks.

"But how are we supposed to flirt to get information if we're here with other guys? Someone might think we're dating them."

Meg furrowed her brow. "They won't have to hang with us. They'll just be nearby if we need help." Despite the fact that they weren't going to "hang with us," they stopped at our table and gave us all delectable grins. Damn them.

Bailey greeted Carina with a kiss on the cheek, and then me. Was that a hint of cologne I detected? Whatever it was, it smelled good. "What are you drinking?" he asked.

I lifted my drink. "This is it for me. I need my brain to work, and I'm driving."

"Are you sure? I can get you something non-alcoholic."

"Positive. I'm fine for now. Thanks."

He turned to ask Finnegan, Meg, and Carina, and they put in their orders. "I'll be back." Bailey made his way to the bar. I wasn't the only one watching him as he went. The ladies at this club had good taste.

Finnegan moved to stand next to me, his hands in his pockets. He gently bumped me with his arm. "I hear you're working on a story tonight. You really love your job."

I hadn't told anyone that I was helping Bellamy because I didn't want to have to explain anything. Also, I didn't know how Finnegan would take it. Would he be offended that Bellamy hadn't asked him and offered to pay him to do it? Or maybe he had? For all I knew, Bellamy had other people on his "consultant" payroll. How silly of me to think I was the first journalist he'd ever trusted. He might get Finnegan to help him all the time.

"Well, once I heard Adam's team was coming here tonight, I

thought easy pickings. I'll just wait another little bit, let them get more grog into their systems." I waggled my brows.

He smiled, his dimples showing. "I doubt you need to wait for the alcohol to take effect. You have other tactics at your disposal." His gaze flicked down to my chest, then quickly back to my eyes. It was speedy, but not speedy enough that I could fool myself that I'd imagined it.

"Work colleagues shouldn't comment on other work colleague's… assets." I chuckled. It wasn't a good idea to flirt with Finnegan, but he made it hard not to. *Note to self: you still have to work with him. Don't make an idiot out of yourself. He's just being silly. Within five minutes of leaving your group, he's going to be eyeing other women and probably taking one home.* Nothing like a reality check to dump a bucket of ice water on your head.

He winked. "Maybe they shouldn't, but sometimes they still do." His smile disappeared. "I didn't really offend you, did I? I'm just mucking around. You know, a joke between friends. Don't worry, Avery; I'd never try to come onto you. You're not the only one who wouldn't want to make things awkward at work." Argh, way to make a girl feel attractive. I shoved the disappointment aside because I didn't really want anything with him. There were so many reasons it would be a bad idea.

I put on my best fake smile and laughed. "Of course you didn't offend me. I knew you were joking. So was I. Well, that got awkward quickly. Sorry, I shouldn't have joked about it." Was I making things worse by going on about it? Argh.

He patted me on the back. "It's fine. We're good. Don't worry." He put his hand out for me to shake. "Definitely friends. Okay?"

I took his hand, his long fingers closing over mine, a jolt of awareness travelling up my arm. I ignored the sensation. "Definitely okay." We shook, and he held my hand longer than was considered normal as he stared into my eyes. I smiled, then extracted my hand. Sometimes a girl had to save herself. He probably had no idea what he was doing to me, and if I wasn't careful, someone, or two some-ones—Meg and Carina—were going to twig onto the fact that I had a wee crush on Finnegan. But then again, I probably had a wee crush on Bailey too. It was all innocent and silly… until someone got made fun of. Bags it not being me tonight. Or ever.

Bailey arrived with the drinks and handed one to Finnegan. I turned to Carina and Meg. "How long do you think we should wait before attempting to gain access to the VIP part?"

Carina looked at Meg. "Twenty minutes? Give them time to relax and down a couple more drinks?"

Meg nodded. "Sounds like a plan. So, Aves, what information are you after, exactly?"

"Looking for who didn't like Adam and who did. Any kind of motivation for murder, really." I explained what I'd found online. I explained what kind of person he was and that he'd cheated on his partner. "I'm thinking it's the girlfriend, or maybe someone trying to protect her. I don't know for sure. There's something going on with the coach, but he's not here that I noticed."

Meg finished her first drink and started on her second. We should probably head upstairs before my friends got drunk. "What do you think's going on with the coach?"

"He might have wanted to get rid of Adam, but I don't know why."

"Why not just fire him?" Carina swayed her hips to the beat as she spoke.

"His uncle donated a ton of money to the club. I don't think he could fire him. Plus, Adam was a good player, so everyone says. Maybe the coach had pressure from more than one place to keep him?" That was something I'd have to look into further. Could Bellamy bring the man in for questioning? He probably already had, but without clear motive, he couldn't delve further, like into emails and stuff. With the information I gave him today, he might just bring him in again, assuming he had before.

Meg had already downed half of her second drink. "Why do these things always have to be hard to figure out?"

"If they were easy, Vinegar would just work it out, and they wouldn't need me." I snorted.

Finnegan looked at me. Having been talking to Bailey, he hadn't been paying attention. "Did I hear my name?" We ladies laughed. He narrowed his eyes. "What?"

Meg pointed at me and grinned. "Avery was just commenting on your sleuthing skills."

My mouth fell open. "Hey, don't blame me." Okay, so it was all me.

His sea-on-a-sunny-day-coloured eyes landed on me. "What about my sleuthing skills?" He wasn't smiling, likely knowing the comment hadn't been favourable.

I mumbled an answer, purposely being hard to understand.

He leaned forward, hand cupped next to his ear. "Pardon? What was that?"

I looked over his shoulder at a woman with a low-cut top and short skirt. "Oh, wow. Look at that!" Everyone turned, and I hurried to the bar to get a glass of water. By the time I got back, they'd be talking about something else.

"Oh, would ya look at that. It's that crazy bitch from the line." Argh! It was the line dancer. She stood with four friends, her arms folded, legs spread wide, her skimpily dressed friends forming a semi-circle behind her. From the frying pan into the fire. Although I didn't get that saying. Being in a hot frying pan was just as deadly as being in a fire. If I was tiny, either one would kill me. I would probably prefer the fire because it would kill me quicker.

I smiled and waved. "Hey, ladies. Having a good night?" I kept my voice happy and chill. Let them think my heart wasn't racing a gazillion miles an hour. If things went south, I'd not only get beaten up, but I'd miss my chance to talk to those football players. Bellamy's future was on the line. Letting him down wasn't an option, not if I wanted to respect myself.

The tallest of her friends stepped forward, into my space. She was at least three inches taller than me, but thankfully, she looked scrawny. Her skinny arms probably weren't very strong. At least that was my hope. "Who the heck do you think you are? No one messes with my friends and gets away with it." She talked the talk. Maybe she had fighting skills? Although her stance was more opportunistic thug than trained fighter. Her hands were fisted at her sides, and she stood flat-footed.

"I hate to ask, but what do you plan on doing to me in here? If you assault me, you'll get kicked out, and I'll press charges." Sometimes talking some sense into people who hadn't thought things through worked.

She stepped close enough that I could feel her body warmth. I wanted to step back to avoid her breath floating down from above, but I didn't want to appear scared. There were a few things I could do to take her down from here. Again, I didn't want to get kicked out. This was a delicate situation. So much for sneaking away from my friends to avoid conflict. Ha ha. "I don't care. You don't know my name. I'll be out of here and away. I always get away with it."

Now I just wanted to teach her a lesson for all those people she wronged. But I wasn't the troublemaker, so the only thing I did was subtly slide my right foot back into fighting stance and rest my palms on my cheeks, my elbows tucked into my body. If she tried anything, my fists didn't have far to go to connect with her face. How did these situations always find me? It wasn't like I was an aggressive person. I just hated bullies and liked to stand up for myself. When I got here and made that vow to myself, I didn't expect that it would cause so much trouble.

"So, you're happy to get kicked out?" I was just making sure. And, no, I didn't plan on going with her. Her aggressive stance had attracted the notice of one of the bouncers, and he was watching.

Her smile was on the evil side. What a sorry excuse for a human, relishing hurting someone else. "Yeah. I love a bit of a fight."

I had my exit strategy. Didn't matter which fist she tried to hit me with, I was going to avoid it, and hopefully make her look stupid doing it. "Look, you can't beat me up. I'd be surprised if you even landed one punch. Rather than embarrass yourself, why don't you turn around and go buy yourself a drink? Chill and enjoy the night." Shame on me for baiting her. I smirked because, well, messing with her tiny brain was fun, and I wanted to see her get kicked out. I didn't know where this Avery had come from, but I was cheering for her.

It was unusual that my friends hadn't come to help, but the club was getting more crowded by the minute, and there were a lot of bodies between me and them. I couldn't spy them through the throng.

Years of hapkido had embedded the mechanics of a fighting body into my brain, so I knew when she was going to move. The look in her eyes became more intense, and her right arm and shoulder moved. It was going to be a pathetic strike because we were so close, and she hadn't rotated her shoulder enough, but I wasn't waiting to see. She raised her right fist. As she threw her punch, I stepped to my left, and pushed her arm away with my left hand, then continued behind her and hurried to meet the bouncer who was striding purposefully towards us. He gave me a quick nod as he passed, indicating that he had it under control, then advance on my would-be attacker. He grabbed her wrist, put a hand on her back, and pushed her towards the door.

When he escorted her past me, I grinned and waved. He he, sucked in.

Two of their group hurried after her, and the original trouble-maker and the friend of hers she'd been in line with stayed, giving me dirty looks. I graced them with another smile, turned, and went back to my friends. Yes, I was a liar—my heart raced, I was sucking in air, and relief that I hadn't been hit swarmed through me—but I wasn't going to show it, and I wasn't going to say anything to anyone.

Carina stared at me. "Where have you been, lady? We were about to send out a search party."

"I needed the bathroom."

Meg chuckled. "Needed to avoid the conversation more like it."

"You're such a poo stirrer." I rolled my eyes.

She sidled up next to me and put her arm around me. "But you love me anyway."

I slitted my eyes. "Do I?"

She pinched my cheek. "Yes. Yes, you do."

I swatted her hand away. "All right. Yes, I do. Happy now? Can you give me a break?"

"I'll think about it." Meg sipped the last of her drink and placed the empty glass on the table. Thankfully, Bailey and Finnegan had let everything else drop and were, in fact, checking out the talent in the room. "Are you ready to ferret out the information?"

"I do believe that I am." Better get it done ASAP before some other drama potentially got me banished from this place.

Meg informed everyone of our intent. Carina got out her phone and typed something into it. "Hang on a minute." After thirty seconds, her phone lit with a message. She smiled. "Bingo! Come wit' me, ladies." I loved having resourceful friends. She must've texted her friend's ex. What a stroke of luck that she knew him.

Bailey looked at Meg. "Be careful. If you need us, text. We'll be around here."

"Thanks, bro." She waved, and off we went, Carina leading the way, the pulsating coloured lights changing her blue hair to purple, then green, then back to blue. She was the coolest person I knew. None of Brad's friends had brightly coloured hair... or nice personalities. Funny how you don't realise at the time how someone you love leaving you can be the best thing that's ever happened. But I knew it now, and that's what mattered.

Dave the rugby player had reached the bouncer at the bottom of the stairs just before we did. He came forward and hugged Carina. His smile seemed genuine. I couldn't hear what he said to her over the music, but they had a small conversation. When they finished, he gestured at all of us to come upstairs. He did a double-take when he saw me, and my eyes widened in pretence that I was surprised to see him too. Then I smiled and waved. My stomach clenched. How would he react?

His shoulders relaxed, and he gave me a closed-mouth smile and chin tip. Phew, it was all good. It would've been deflating to be turned away at the eleventh hour. Sure, I could get information tomorrow, or the next day, but it would've involved a lot more legwork and time. Time Bellamy didn't have. I also had to consider how peed off Adam would be after I exiled him for twenty-four hours. Hopefully, he wasn't getting more powerful as a poltergeist while he was away. If only I knew how these things worked.

How would everyone else react? I swallowed as we reached the top of the stairs.

Most, if not all, of the players were there, lounging around on couches, drinks in hand, a couple of the guys with women in their laps. Peta, the manager, and Cath walked over. Cath blinked when she realised who I was, well I was assuming she just realised. I gave her a tentative smile and leaned closer so she and Peta could hear what I said. "Hi. I was here tonight with my friend, and she heard that Dave was here. They're old friends. I'm here to have a good time, not for work."

Cath gave me a sad smile. "Oh, that's good. I'm sick of talking about everything, if you know what I mean."

"I do. I promise no questions from me tonight. You've been through enough." I should buy them both a drink, show them I was socialising rather than working.

Peta wasn't as easy to navigate. "I'm not sure you should be up here with us. If Mr Atherton finds out…." She gave Dave a pointed look.

Dave grinned. "If no one tells him, he won't know. Besides, she's not going to ask any questions, and we're not going to talk about anything." He moved his gaze to me. "Am I right?"

My smile was conspiratorial. "You are so right. All I want to do is drink and dance." I looked at Peta. "Why don't I buy you and Cath a drink as a show of good faith. We'll make a toast to having a good night." If I could've secretly crossed my fingers, I would have.

Peta dragged her gaze over my friends, then back to me. She huffed. "Fine, but if I hear anything about Adam coming out of your mouth, you're banished to commoners' land. Am I clear? No killing our vibe."

I gave her a firm nod. "I'm not a vibe killer. You're clear as. Shall we order drinks?" I raised my brows in question.

"Sure." Her upturned lips were barely a smile, but it was better than nothing. The thing was, she was right to be wary. Smart lady. I had my work cut out for me.

Thanks to my blue-haired friend's witty sense of humour and Meg's good looks, it didn't take long for the players to invite us to sit with them. Carina was the centre of attention, and Meg had three guys hanging onto her every shouted word. The music couldn't have been louder—the bass vibrated the floor. Not that I was the biggest party animal, but it made me want to dance. Unfortunately, I wasn't here for that. I pretended to sip my second alcoholic beverage. Not drinking would make me look way out of place.

Hmm… interesting. I listened to a player called Errol talk about his love of craft beer. He and his family liked to brew their own. But that wasn't what was interesting. At a couch on the other side of the room, Dave and Cath snuggled together, stared into each other's eyes, and generally looked like they were really into each other. And there was the passionate kiss, confirming they were more than just friends. Was this new? Had Dave had his eye on her the whole time she was dating Adam? Or were they just comforting each other after someone they cared about had died? I had all the questions and no answers. This job could be so frustrating sometimes.

My bag vibrated. I'd put my phone on vibrate because I was never going to hear my phone pinging or ringing over club music. I pulled it out of my bag and grinned. Too funny. Finnegan had sent a message—a picture of him and Bailey pulling faces. Another message came through. *Are you missing us yet?*

I sent back: *Who dis? How did you get my number?* I giggled at my own joke. He he.

After a bit, another text came through: a picture of Finnegan and Bailey looking out of sorts. Their unimpressed faces were adorable.

"Work with me here. It's not good for a guy's ego when the lady he's talking to would rather chat on her phone."

Oops. I looked up. Errol had a hand on his heart and a sweet smile on his face. "Sorry. A couple of my friends are being stupid. Sorry. Your craft beer sounds awesome. Do you ever sell it?"

"We've approached a few pubs, but no luck yet. We might need to refine it. I feel like it'll happen sooner rather than later."

"That's awesome. Good on you." How to turn the conversation to team politics. And then I spied someone that would help me get at least some information without actually looking like I was asking.

I put on a bit of a ditzy voice. "Oh, is that Byron over there? I thought he'd be too young to come out. And isn't he just a helper at the club? It's so lovely that you include him. You guys are so nice." If I'd been drinking something, I would've spit it out because Errol sat up straighter and puffed his chest out. Seriously, that's all it took to make a guy happy? One measly compliment? Maybe he needed better friends and family.

"Not usually, but he finally got called up this afternoon after training. He's been waiting for a spot in this team for a while, and Coach decided now was a good time. They don't want to replace Adam with a more experienced player yet." His mouth curved down. "You know... it's too soon. We don't need someone else trying to fill Adam's spot. He was one of a kind. It's going to take a while to figure out new team dynamics."

"Oh, yeah. I'm so sorry about that. You guys must be so close. I hope you find your magic again. And Byron seems like a good kid."

"Yeah, he's always willing to please. Anything the coach says, he gets onto straight away. And he's not bad on the field. With a bit of experience, he'll be good." He looked at his empty glass. "I need another one of these. Can I get you anything?"

"Oh, thanks, but I'm fine." I held up my glass, which had been three-quarters full for the last thirty minutes.

"I'll be back." He got up and left. Now who to chat to? Dave and Cath were very cosy on a couch. His tongue was down her throat. Lovely. Maybe I'd chat to them later. Intruding on their love-fest was a bit gross and probably a bit creepy since I hardly knew them. I imagined walking over there and standing in front of them, waiting for them to finish what they were doing so I could chat. I laughed.

"Do you often sit by yourself and laugh?"

I looked up. It was Quiet Nodder, one of the players who'd avoided speaking to me so far. I smiled. "Hey. Um, I would say no, but that would be a lie."

"Mind if I sit?"

"Not at all."

The muscled blond sat next to me. "Thanks. I'm Xavier."

"I'm Avery, but I suspect you already know that. How're you enjoying the night?" Argh, small talk, my most-hated pastime, except it could lead to big talk, which I needed. And why wasn't that expression invented yet. If there was small talk, why wasn't there big talk? I shook my head. There was no time to get lost in my maze of a brain. It had been a long day, and I clearly needed a break.

He leaned back and crossed his legs, placing one ankle on the other knee. "It's okay. Coach Atherton wanted us to reset, relax, whatever after the recent... drama. I'm just not into it though. It's been a long and emotional week."

"Were you and Adam close?" I asked as innocently as possible. "If you'd rather not answer, that's fine. I'm not actually pumping you for information." Lie. "Anything we talk about here won't go anywhere near the newspaper. I promise. You just look like you need someone to talk to."

He gave me a lopsided grin. "Can I get that in writing."

I chuckled. "Sure. Got a piece of paper? I've got a pen." I grabbed one of the many I had in my bag and held it up.

"Ha, of course you're carrying a pen." He patted his front jeans pockets. "'Fraid I'm all out of paper. I'll have to take your word for it. Besides, I have a good nose for people, and you seem okay."

"Thanks. It must be hard training when the team's so down."

As he spoke, his gaze wandered the room, floating from one group of players to another. "You would think, but everyone's not as sad as I thought they would be. I mean, some of them are, but not everyone." That would've normally been my cue to ask if he was one of the ones who wasn't upset, but I wasn't supposed to be probing, so I let it go.

"How long have you been playing rugby?" It was time to build our rapport and for me to get to know him on a personal level.

"Since I was a young kid. My grandpa and I often went to games together. I've always loved it. With his encouragement, I started playing when I was seven, but it wasn't always easy. Most of the guys are cool now, but coming up the ranks as a teenager, it was hard being gay. It's a real lad's sport, and there were a lot of closed minds. I tried to hide who I was, but I wasn't always successful, and

it took a toll on my mental health. Thankfully, things changed…
mostly." He sipped his drink and stared at one particular group of
players who looked glummer than everyone else. Four of them. I'd
sneak a photo later, then look them up. Were they Adam's core
friend group in the team? Had they also given Xavier a hard time
about being gay? Why couldn't everyone just accept people for who
they were? People made me sad.

"Are those guys not included in the 'mostly' group?"

He turned his head to look at me. "Yes. So, what brings an
Aussie to England?" So, end of that line of information, but he'd
given me enough to start with, so that was good. Maybe I'd go flirt
with those buffoons later, commiserate with them over the death of
such an awesome player.

"I had nothing better to do." He raised a brow at my non-
answer, and I grinned. Fair was fair—he'd given me some insight
into his life; it was my turn to reciprocate. "A bad relationship
ended, and my parents aren't my biggest supporters. I'm better off
as far away from them as possible. I figured a new start here was just
the thing, and turns out, it is."

"How long have you been here?"

"A couple of months." I blinked. Was that all? Struth. It seemed
like a year. All the things I'd been through already…. How had it
only been such a short time?

"Seems like you've settled in well already. I've read a couple of
your articles, actually, and you've obviously made some friends." He
lifted his glass towards Meg and Carina.

"Yeah, it's been better than I could've imagined. It's the best
thing I've ever done, to be honest, moving here." I almost, almost
said I'd cyberstalked him and was sorry about how Adam had
treated him, but that wasn't a conversation I wanted to have. Maybe
I'd regret it later, but I didn't want him to think I thought he had a
motive for killing Adam—that would imply I thought he might have
done it, and from the vibes I got, he was a great guy. In another
time and place, maybe we'd be friends. He was certainly easy to talk
to. Was I not doing my job right now, leaving a loose end that might
come back to bite Bellamy? Possibly. But surely he wasn't a

murderer. He spoke of his unjust treatment with sadness rather than anger.

He smiled. "That's great. I'm so glad it's working out for you."

Three of the players approached. One of them was the player with the curly red hair, beard, blue eyes, and freckles that Byron had looked at weirdly when I was at the field. One of the other ones didn't bother looking at me. He went straight to Xavier. "Hey, wanna go dance?"

Xavier looked at me. "Do you want to come?"

"Ah, no, it's fine. I'm not much of a dancer." I wasn't the first one to hit the dance floor, but I did like it. Another white lie to add to my tally. When I died, the portal that opened for me was so not going to be the white-light one. "I might see what Meg's up to."

The red-headed guy looked at me. "You don't have to do that. I'm not much of a dancer either. Thought I might chat to you while the lads go downstairs."

I shrugged. "Okay, fine." I smiled at Xavier. "Have fun. I'll see you later."

"Yeah, for sure."

Red-headed guy sat next to me. "I'm Joel."

"Hi, Joel. I'm Avery. How's it going?" How long was it going to take before he got to why he wanted to talk to me. Either he was going to give me information on Adam, or he was going to ask for my number. I doubted it was the latter.

He stared at my cleavage for a moment before looking at my face. "Not great, to be honest. Adam's death has shaken me up. I know you're looking into it for the paper, so thank you for trying to get to the bottom of it. I saw Coach Atherton shooing you away." He leaned towards me and spoke in a low voice, not that anyone else was going to hear anything with the overpowering music volume. In fact, I was having to squint to hear him… and yes, I was aware that made no sense, but my body did what it did to help. "I think he knows who did it and is protecting them." He looked over at Dave and Cath. Interesting.

He turned back to me, and I met his determined gaze. "Are you sure? Have you told the police?"

"Not yet. I only figured it out tonight. As soon as I realised, I thought I'd better tell you. I mean, what if I die in a car crash on the way home or something? Then the truth will never come out. I'll head to the station in the morning. I'm a bit over the limit right now, and maybe they won't believe me. Plus, I don't have any actual proof. All I know is that Adam deserves better than this." His eyes slid to my breasts again. And this was why I didn't wear revealing tops. I could read people better when I could look into their eyes when talking to them.

"Oh, okay." Dare I get my hopes up, or was this a personal vendetta? Was he even smart enough to work it out? Wouldn't a clever person be in a taxi on the way to the police right now or at least on the phone to them? "Who do you think did it, and why?"

He chugged his beer, draining it. "Hang on." He burped, got up, and went to the bar. Mmm, charming. *I'll just wait here for you to get back.* I looked around. Meg met my eyes from across the room where she was chatting to two of the players and Peta. She grinned and gave me a thumbs up. I reciprocated. I wasn't sure if she meant she was having a good time and was I, or if she meant she was getting some good intel. It wasn't long before Joel returned. It was handy having your own VIP bar. He plonked down next to me, the thump reverberating through the couch. A splash of beer leaped out of the glass and onto his crotch, making him look like he'd wet himself. He ignored it. Obviously an experienced drunk, he didn't much care. "As I was saying."

"Please, go on."

He lowered his voice and leaned over, his yeasty breath dampening the side of my face. It took everything in me not to make an "ew" face and move away. "Don't look because you'll make it obvious, but Dave and Cath over there. They're in on it. What's it been, two or three days, and she's already rooting someone else. They must've been cheating on Adam and wanted him out of the way."

Did I believe it? I wasn't sure, but I was going along with it, if for no other reason than sympathizing with Joel would get more out of him. "Oh, wow, that's horrible. What a betrayal. Poor Adam. Which one of them do you think stabbed him?"

"Cath is good with knives, but I don't think she's strong enough. She probably told Dave what to do, I reckon. Stabbed in the back twice, he was. Once to kill him, and once when those cheaters got together." His eyes did their best to stay on my face, but my boobs won out, attracting his attention. Maybe I should draw a smiley face on them; then he wouldn't have to look at my face at all.

"Why wouldn't Cath just leave him? Why kill him?" So far, all I heard was his assumptions. I didn't want to chase false leads.

"He paid all their bills. Dave hasn't got much money and still lives with his parents. Plus, he's been trying to get back at Adam since Adam slept with his sister, then ghosted her."

The plot thickened. "When was that?"

"About five months ago."

"While he was still living with Cath?"

"Yeah, so what?" Wow, the guy didn't get double standards. At this point, Dave was looking like the good older brother. But he also didn't like Adam. Was that enough of a motive for murder?

"Sleeping with his sister and ghosting her doesn't seem like a good enough reason to kill someone. Would that be enough for you to kill someone?"

He shrugged. "I don't have a sister, but probably not. Doesn't mean he didn't do it. A lad shouldn't move on with his mate's girlfriend when he's not even in the ground yet." He swore and mumbled something about Cath's reputation, and it started with an s and rhymed with shut. Charming.

"Won't your coach be angry if he finds out you spoke to me?"

"He won't know if we don't tell him." He grinned at my boobs. They weren't amused. His face twisted into anger. "Besides, he and Adam had a couple of arguments just before he died. Adam wouldn't tell me what they were about, but Coach wasn't happy, so I don't know that Coach will care about who killed him as much as me. We were best mates, you know. I've lost my best mate." He slumped back into the couch, and I almost felt sympathy for him.

"I'm sorry, Joel. What happened to Adam is terrible, and I know you must be upset. I'll look into what you told me, okay? And I'll make sure the coach doesn't find out." What had they been fighting about? I could ask Adam about it, which meant I couldn't just banish him tomorrow morning. He hadn't mentioned anything about the coach, so maybe they weren't arguing about anything that important.

Byron wandered over. He smiled. "I hope everything's going okay over here." His gaze went from me to Joel and stayed there. Joel's mopey face made it look like I was terrible company. Thanks, Joel.

The redhead looked up at his teammate. "Yeah, just peachy. It's just like you to check up and make sure everyone's okay. You're a good 'un, Lappy. Always getting us everything we need." Lappy? Was his last name Lapland or something?

The light wasn't great up here, but I was sure Byron's jaw bunched, and frustration flickered in his eyes. "Yeah, I'm a good one. Coach likes it when we look out for each other. Teamwork. You know."

"Ha, yeah, teamwork." Joel tipped the rest of his beer into his mouth. "I need another. Look after her for me while I'm gone." He lumbered to his feet and headed to the bar. Look after me for him? What was that supposed to mean?

"He's not giving you any *problems*, is he?" I wasn't a 100 per cent sure what Byron meant, but I could guess. Peta watched our exchange from near the bar. Had she sent Byron to make sure Joel wasn't spilling any team secrets or secrets about her friend Cath?

"Joel hasn't done anything inappropriate. It's cool." Other than stare at my boobs way too much.

"Good. Coach doesn't like scandals, and I know you're a jour-nalist. I mean, not that I want him to do anything to any other woman either, but you know, I have to look out for them. They don't always make the best decisions." He snapped his mouth shut, maybe realising he'd said too much.

Byron wasn't drunk that I could tell, and he was on alert because I was a journalist, but maybe he'd let something else slip if I gave him the chance. "It's fine. Joel was just telling me how upset he is that Adam's gone. He said you're on the team now though, so congrats. I'm surprised you're not drinking it up."

He looked around, then back at me. "Someone's gotta keep an eye on this lot, and I'm used to it. With everything that's happened, me and Peta have to make sure the boys are okay. We brought a minibus. I'll drive most of them home, make sure they get there in one piece."

How did he feel having to run around after them? "Are they going to get someone else in to do your former job?"

"Yeah, the guy starts on Monday."

"That's great. You'll need all your energy for training and playing, I would imagine. It's such an exciting step."

He grinned, the first unguarded expression he'd given me. "Yeah. I've waited a long time for this opportunity." His shoulders sagged with his smile. "Except, I would've loved to play while Adam was still captain. He was a wiz on the field. The team won't be the same without him." He eyed the couch.

"Feel free to sit here. We don't have to talk about rugby. Do you work, or are you studying?" He was so wary, probably because he was the only sober one in the team right now, and he knew I wanted more of a story. "I think you could do with a break from babysitting."

He laughed. "Yeah, I s'pose I could." He sat but lingered on the edge of the seat, not quite ready to get comfortable with our conversation.

"So, work or study, or both?"

"I'm studying at the moment. In my second year of uni and living with my parents. What about you? What brings an Australian to England?"

As I gave him an abridged version of my life events, Carina and Meg came over and advised that they were going down to dance. Two of the better-looking players waited for them at the stairs. "Do you want to come?" asked Meg.

I smirked. "Five's a crowd. Have fun."

Carina grinned and grabbed Meg's hand. "Come on, lovie. Those hotties won't wait forever." Off they went. I smiled. At least Meg was having some fun. Since her boyfriend had moved away, I hadn't seen her let loose and enjoy herself. Tonight would be good for her.

I sipped my drink, and we chitchatted for a few minutes, or maybe it was longer. I couldn't tell. A dizzy spell hit me. I shut my eyes and centred myself, but it didn't help. When I opened my eyes, the dizziness had passed, but everything felt... weird.

Byron peered at me. "You're exceptionally good at your job, aren't you." He wasn't bad-looking.

I giggled and leaned against him. It seemed like a good idea to put my hand on his thigh, so I did. Was it a good idea? I wasn't sure, but he didn't remove it. Fatigue swept over me, and I wanted to close my eyes. The dizziness returned. "Um, yeah. I don't feel so well." Had the chicken dinner been off? Or had I had beef for dinner? Hmm.... I tried to sip my drink again, but my mouth missed the straw. I laughed. "Oopsie."

Byron put his hand on my knee. Aw, how nice. "I've read all your articles. You've even helped solved a crime, haven't you?"

I swayed. It took all my effort to put my glass on the table so I didn't drop it all over myself. Didn't want to look like I wet myself like Joel. I giggled. "Ha, crimes are my thing. Love 'em." Ha, that was funny too. I laughed.

"What's so funny?" Byron's forehead wrinkled, but he was smiling.

"Noth... noth... ing." Hmm, my lips were numb, and my tongue didn't want to work. I closed my eyes for a moment. Food poisoning or something else? I couldn't think it through, but fear broke through the wooliness. Had someone spiked my drink? I tried to get my phone out of my bag so I could text someone. I wasn't sure who. But I knew I needed to let someone know. My fingers wouldn't do what I asked them. My head lolled back on the couch, useless.

Byron's voice came through the haze. "Avery, are you okay? How much have you had to drink? Avery?"

I think I mumbled something, but I wasn't sure what. Joel was suddenly in front of me, helping me stand. Did Byron just tell someone he saw me take some tablets with my alcohol? What? I opened my eyes, but the room swam as we moved through it. I tried to tell people I hadn't had too much, but all that came out was some slurred sounds. Way, way inside my brain, I watched. The little voice that couldn't come out told me that I'd been drugged. But why, and by who? Would Byron look after me, or had he done it? No one would drug me. Surely Avery was just being a silly possum. A chortle gurgled in my throat.

Ooh, a door. Peta opened it. Joel practically carried me through. Byron told Peta I was a mess, but I wanted to go home with Joel. Did I say that? Maybe, but who knew? Oh, well.

Byron was still talking. Ooh, he didn't want me seen with the players because of the other incidents so he was going to put me in an Uber and send me home with Joel. Peta said it was a good idea— at least, I think she did. Words were hard to hold onto, sound flitting away before I could snatch meaning from it. The door clunked shut. The floor sloped, and my feet couldn't work out where they were supposed to go. The ground kept moving out of the way or jumping up to meet my feet.

"It's okay, Avery. I've got you. That a girl." Joel.

The music became muffled. We floated down, down, down. My head throbbed.

Molasses thoughts oozed through me. Where was I, and what was I doing? Wanted sleep. I melted into the floor. Reality was an indecipherable concept. There was nothing left but a bubbling pit of ebony.

Turning away from the spark of light inside, it's sharp brightness too much, I surrendered. A black blob of goo returning to its origin. I was no more.

CHAPTER 17

Before I opened my eyes, I knew something was off. And it wasn't just the pounding headache. I felt like I was in bed, but it wasn't my bed. My bed wasn't this soft and comfortable. How much had I drunk? I tried to think back to last night, but it was like digging through wet clay. Heavy eyelids weren't enough to stop me. It was time to face the truth of whether I'd had a one-night stand I didn't remember.

The room was faintly lit. I lay on my side facing a bedside table and wall. An open door was on the wall near the foot of the bed, brighter light coming from it. I slowly rolled over, doing my best to stay quiet. My limbs complained. Why were my muscles sore? Eventually I faced the other way.

My stomach clenched.

I wasn't alone.

The other person sat up. "Avery, are you okay?"

The building horror dissipated. The light hadn't been enough to identify the person, but her voice was. "Carina?"

She leaned over and turned on her bedside lamp before turning back and staring at my face. "T'ank goodness you're awake. How are you feeling?"

I licked my bottom lip. "I could do with some water. I'm afraid to ask, but what in Hades happened last night? This doesn't look like your bedroom." In fact, my brain got itself into second gear, and I realised whose it was. I wasn't sure if it was better or worse. "Why are we in Vinegar's bedroom. Seriously, what happened last night? Please don't tell me Vinegar and I—"

She laughed. "Oh, God no! Finny slept in his spare room, and we didn't do anyt'ing eid'er." She winked. "Look." She threw the covers off us. We were dressed in last night's outfits, sans shoes, of course.

"Why aren't I in my own bed? Why aren't you? Did we bring the party back here?"

She gave me a sad look that also managed to say "Sorry I have to tell you this." "Do you remember anyt'ing about last night?"

I shut my eyes. Yesterday. What had I done yesterday? I opened my eyes. "I went to the rugby club, and they told me to leave. Ooh, we went out for dinner. I remember getting to the club after that. We made it upstairs to the players."

"What else?"

"Um…. I need a minute. Hang on." I shut my eyes again and took some slow, deep breaths. I visualised myself walking up those stairs. Her friend's ex was one of the players. That's right. I managed to get to the bit where the girls asked me to dance with them. "You and Meg went dancing, and I didn't want to. Things get fuzzy after that." I swallowed the spike of fear that clogged my throat.

"Avery, you're awake!" Finnegan stood inside the doorway. He wore navy-blue-tartan pyjama shorts and a white T-shirt. Even in my current groggy state, I couldn't help but appreciate his muscled legs and chest. His toned arms filled out the sleeves, too, and the only word I could think of was sexy. I'd have to be dead not to notice. He strode into the room and sat on the end of the bed. "How are you feeling?"

Lying down felt too intimate—which was stupid because Carina was in the room, too, but it was what it was, so I sat up. "Did I do a gym class I don't remember?"

"What?" Carina looked at me, puzzled.

"My muscles are sore. I'm exhausted. I'm sure I didn't drink that much." I wasn't stupid, and my addled brain was finally putting two and two together. Heart racing, I asked, "Was I drugged?"

Carina rubbed my back. "Yes, we t'ink so, but not'ing happened while you were out of it."

I swallowed, tears of relief burning my eyes.

Finnegan edged his way along the bed, closer to me. The way he was looking at me…. It was as if he wanted to give me a hug. But he didn't. Instead, my legs were stretched out under the covers, and he put his hand on my ankle and squeezed. "Everything's going to be okay. When we found you, we took you to the hospital, and they took bloods and a urine sample. They said you might not remember going, depending on what they drugged you with. You were pretty out of it."

Carina and Finnegan shared a look. The fear returned.

"What did I do? Did I get undressed or something?"

"Not'ing like d'at." She looked at Finnegan. "We should tell her. It's not her fault."

Finnegan gave me a kind smile. "It's not terrible. I'll start with how we found you. Peta, the manager with the rugby team, came to find Meg and Carina as soon as she saw you leaving with one of the players."

Carina nodded. "Yeah, she's a good one. She knew you'd want us to know—ladies don't just leave d'eir lady friends wit'out telling them where d'ere going. She found us on the dance floor. D'en we raced outside. I called Finny, and he and Bailey rushed out. We found you outside wit' one of d'e players, a redhead… Joel. He claimed he was waiting wit' you for an Uber and was trying to get you home safe."

Fire ignited in Finnegan's eyes, and his jaw muscles bunched. "We all know that was a lie."

None of us said anything. I knew what he was implying—I'd narrowly avoided being raped. Nausea washed through me. Even through the exhaustion and brain fog, anger followed the sick feeling. I swore, and I never swore.

Carina grabbed my hand and squeezed. "I know, love. We said plenty of d'at last night."

"I'm so sorry, Lightning, but because we can't prove anything, and nothing else happened to you, the police won't be able to do anything. When the test results are back, we can let them know, but other than that, there won't be any follow up. The VIP area doesn't have video surveillance. There's no way of proving who drugged you. The police could even say you did it to yourself by accident."

My chin dropped to my chest, and I closed my eyes. Could this get any worse? Being a victim and being blamed was horrific. How did people get through things like this? "And I can't even remember everyone I spoke to. It could've been anyone up there." I was so stupid. "How did I let this happen?" A tear escaped one eye and slid down my cheek. I kept my head down so they wouldn't see. My parents were right—I was a clueless idiot playing at things I wasn't equipped for. I couldn't tell Bellamy. He'd never let me help them again.

"Hey, it's okay. It wasn't your fault. You know d'at, logically, right?" Carina's soothing voice didn't make me feel any better, but I wasn't going to go on about it. They'd had to babysit me as it was.

I wiped the tear away and raised my head. "Thank you both for looking out for me and having me here, making sure I was all right. You guys are the best." *And I don't deserve friends as good as you.*

Finnegan gave me a gorgeous smile. "You're one of us now—a reporter at the *Manesbury Daily*, and a Manesburian. We'll always have your back, won't we, Car?"

"You bet. Which brings me to what you did. You're a Band-Aid person, aren't you, Aves?"

It took a minute for my cotton-wool brain to catch up. "Ah, yeah. Rip it off. Whatever it is, I'd rather find out from you two than Joystick."

They both guffawed. "D'at's your name for Joy? It's apt."

I grinned. "It was Joyless, but when I found out her last name, well, it wrote itself."

Finnegan was the first to stop laughing. "I think you can tell her. I'll go and make breakfast." He stared into my eyes. "I'm glad you're all right. I'll call Bailey too. He and Meg were beside themselves last night. They came to the hospital too." He paused for a moment, maybe disputing whether to say something else. "Um, I wouldn't normally say anything, but, well, Bailey was really freaked out. He often talks about you too. I think he's into you, Lightning, and you know what? He's a great guy. You could do way worse." His grin, for some reason, was self-deprecating. Okay. This was all too much with a headache and missing memory.

"Um, thanks. He's awesome, but like I've told everyone a gazillion times, I'm not looking at dating anyone for the foreseeable future. My life is complicated enough as it is. Last night being a prime example. I can't even look after myself, let alone be a decent partner for someone else. Besides, I'm enjoying being there for myself. I'm lucky I have all of you—Meg and Bailey included. I've never had people who really cared about me before, so thanks." Oh, jeez, I was embarrassing myself. "Sorry for oversharing."

Carina smiled. "Lady, you should overshare more often. It's okay to lean on your friends, you know?"

"I'm learning."

Finnegan got up. "I'll call you when breakfast is ready."

After he left, Carina cleared her throat. "Okay, so, don't be embarrassed because you were off your face, and you didn't know what you were saying. We all took it with a grain of salt."

Hades, what had I said? My cheeks heated before I even knew. God, please don't let my secret crushes be out in the open. "Band-Aid, please." Against my better judgement, I didn't slap my hands over my ears and yell, "La, la, la, la, la, la."

"Bailey drove your car. You were in the back in between me and Finny. You snuggled against him and told him you loved him, and then you said the same thing to Bailey. You told them they were both super hot and you'd *do* them." She pressed her lips together, but they curled up anyway, and her eyes watered. She was totally trying not to laugh.

Oh my God, oh my God, this was worse than I thought. I swore… again, and my face was on fire. "I'm going to die. You do realise this means I have to move back to Australia. I can't show my face in England ever again."

"If it makes you feel any better, they laughed about it, and when we got to the hospital, you hit on the young doctor too. You told him you loved him. The guys were much put out d'at your affection wasn't just for d'em." This time she did laugh.

Time for damage control. "You know I didn't mean it, right?" She looked at me like she didn't believe it. "I mean, they're both gorgeous men. I can't deny that, but I don't love either of them, and if I really wanted to sleep with them, I would've made moves. This is just so wrong. They're my friends, and I want nothing more."

She grinned. "It's okay, lovie; we know. Meg's been trying to get you and Bailey toged'er for ages, and you won't budge. I'm sure the guys t'ought it was sweet. They'd be so lucky to have a woman like you after d'em. There's not'ing to be embarrassed about."

"Says you, the woman who wasn't throwing herself at all the men last night." I shook my head, which was a mistake, as my headache throbbed worse. "At least that player didn't get me alone." I shuddered. "What was his name again?"

"Joel. We took a photo of him. I'll show you later, maybe jog your memory."

"When do my results come back?" I wanted to know what that dirtbag had given me. How dare he! Scum bucket.

"A few days. We can go to the police when we find out."

My eyes widened. "No!"

Her forehead wrinkled. "Why d'e hell not?"

I took a deep breath, then spoke quietly, "Don't say anything, especially to Vinegar, but Sergeant Bellamy asked me to help solve this case. He knew I was going to try and get more information, and he told me to be careful. If he finds out, he'll never ask for my help again." She opened her mouth and shut it. Good. She understood. "I know it's stupid. And I know it's dangerous to have these pigs running around spiking drinks, but maybe I can get them another way. I'm still not thinking clearly, but there's an idea forming. I'll tell you about it when I figure it out. And do not tell Vinegar about this."

"Why not?"

"I doubt he'd like his dad's best friend asking me to help instead of him. I don't want to upset him, and I don't want to make it harder for me to get let in at the station in the future. Please? Look, maybe I'll change my mind in a few days if I can't remember anything, but I need a chance to fix this before we tell anyone. Okay?"

She huffed. "You're putting me in a difficult position, lady." She twirled a lock of blue hair around her finger as she thought it through. "Argh, okay. But you've only got t'ree days. After d'at, we'll have anod'er talk about it."

I didn't like that much, but it was better than nothing. "Okay, deal."

"Come on. Let's have breakfast before Finny comes looking for us."

Over breakfast, I convinced Finnegan not to tell Bellamy. I used the excuse that he had a lot on his plate with the Adam murder case. I promised I'd follow it up later. Another little lie. It wasn't till I'd said goodbye to Carina and Finnegan and locked myself in my flat that it really hit home. Someone had almost raped me. If it hadn't been for my friends, who knew, I could even be dead right now. What I couldn't work out was whether it was because I was a journalist looking into Adam's murder, or it was something those players did because they got off on it.

Whatever it was, I was going to figure it out, and when I did, whoever was in on this was going to wish they'd never met me.

Game on.

CHAPTER 18

I slept on and off on Sunday, and when I went to bed for the final time, my memory hadn't returned. It was more than frustrating because there might be information I forgot that could've helped solve Adam's murder. At least when I awoke on Monday morning, I was feeling much better, and whilst I couldn't remember much more, I'd had weird dreams that might help.

Once dressed, I sat at the kitchen table with my coffee and laptop. Bellamy had texted me last night because I hadn't contacted him. I told him I had a bad case of food poisoning and I'd get back to him Monday afternoon.

I had work to do.

Even though I couldn't remember everything about last night, I knew the whole team had been there, and Cath was definitely there. Hmm. I think Peta was, too, but that wasn't clear. Oh, that's right; Carina and Finnegan had told me she found the girls and told them I needed help. So she was there. But I couldn't recall seeing her. "Argh!" I gritted my teeth against the tears that wanted to invade. I wasn't going to cry. Those mould-eating parasites were not going to get the better of me. I was okay. The helplessness at being drugged and the shame that I'd let it happen was offset by the fact that they hadn't gotten their way. My friends had saved me. I owed them big time. And Peta. Thank Hades she decided to do the right thing.

Other than Peta, had anyone else known that Joel was taking me home? Did he drug me? I couldn't recall even talking to him. I'd held my drink most of the time. At least I probably did. I huffed. I didn't even know that. This was what it felt like to be a baby. To have no control over your memory, your brain. The pitch-black hole that was much of last night was a piece of hell, sucking my attention even now. The sooner I let it go, the better, but… it was so hard. I grabbed my scalp and dug my fingers in. "Remember, damn you, Avery."

I sucked in a deep breath, let it out, and took a fortifying sip of coffee. Beating myself up wasn't going to help. Maybe I'd feel better if I could crack this case. I looked up each player's social media. Likely most of them didn't know what happened, but maybe one or two others would. In that case, they probably hadn't been told not to post on social media. There could be evidence in their pictures.

I started with the players I couldn't remember even seeing. Joel wouldn't be so stupid as to post photos of himself or me, surely, if he'd planned to hurt me. Or maybe he did take photos of us smiling and looking happy so he could say, "Look, she was all over me. She wanted to go home with me."

Instagram was first on my list of places to check. I went through each player, and bingo! I was in the background of two selfies. At one stage sitting on the couch with Joel. I was leaning towards him, but I wasn't all over him. My shoulders loosened slightly. At least I wasn't in his lap and slobbering all over him. The second photo I found, I was sitting on the couch still, but Joel wasn't there—Byron was. I had my hand on his thigh, and I was leaning against his shoulder, my eyes half closed. *Noooooo! I don't remember that. That's not right.* My throat burned with more tears I refused to shed.

What else had I done that I didn't remember and that my friends hadn't seen?

When I'd showered yesterday, I'd looked over every inch of my body I could see. There was a bruise on one shin, and bruises on my upper arms. Maybe those were from Joel holding me up when I couldn't walk properly? My thighs weren't bruised, and it didn't feel like anything else had happened, but I couldn't be sure. But then again, if Peta had told Meg and Carina quickly, there wouldn't have been time for anything to happen in a room somewhere at the club.

Take a deep breath, Avery.

I hugged myself and dug my fingers into my arms to stave off the rising panic. My breaths came faster. I shut my mouth and took deliberate breaths through my nose. "Don't lose it now." My voice wavered. That wasn't good enough. If I was going to take myself away from the raging emotional waters, I needed to be firmer. "You're okay, Avery. Nothing happened. You'll be fine. Just catch these smears of human excrement."

That brought a different kind of fear. It was something I'd been avoiding, but I couldn't any longer.

It was time to talk to Adam.

And I couldn't do it in the street. I rubbed my temples. I was going to have to invite him into my personal space, but there was no way I was letting him into my home. It was going to have to be my car.

I spent another thirty minutes looking at social media and found a couple more pictures to help me piece my night together. That done, it was time to take another risk. Adam.

I didn't have any interviews booked today. Other than work on this case, my plan had been to get back to the murder of the candlemaker's husband and do a fluffy (pardon the pun) article on the dog-grooming salon at Cramptonbury. I also promised Meg and Bailey I'd have lunch at the pub and let them know how I was doing. So I packed my laptop and dressed in a denim above-the-knee skirt and green T-shirt. My banishing crystal nestled safely in my tight fist. I should get it put on a chain so I could always have it next to my skin. Silly me for not realising how much I'd need it.

At the bottom of the stairs, I stopped and took a deep breath. Before I lost my nerve, I opened the door. Adam couldn't touch me while I was on the property, so I had time to turn and lock the door.

Even if he could touch me here, I'd probably lock the door because Mrs Crabby was just as scary, if not more so than any poltergeist.

The ghost wasn't standing at the front fence. Nevertheless, I didn't drop my guard. My stomach clenched as I opened the gate and stepped out.

Goosebumps raced up my arms. An invisible shower of fury pelted me. My eyes widened, and my nostrils flared. I jerked my head around, looking for the source. The crystal dug painfully into my palm as my fist tightened.

He was coming. And he was pissed.

It took another half a minute or so for him to fade in. That was different. He didn't just pop into existence like ghosts usually did. Finally, he appeared solid. He stared at me, hatred burning from his eyes. "Don't banish me again, dammit! You have no idea what you're doing to me."

I made sure my voice was strong—if he had any indication I was the least bit scared, he might attack. What that would entail, I had no idea, and I didn't want to find out. "I'm not going to this time unless you do something to hurt me. Maybe consider not leaving dead rats as a warning."

He didn't say okay or admit any wrongdoing. What else did I expect from a narcissist? "Have you found my killer yet?"

Mrs Crabby called from the front porch, "What in the dickens are you doing, silly girl? You'll set the town talking with that crazy behaviour."

Oh. My. Lord. Why hadn't I gone straight to the car? Adam would've found me. The fear and seeing him and him being annoying... it made me forget where I was and who was watching. I turned and smiled. "Morning. I'm... um... talking to the universe. I knew how upset you were about the rats, and I thought if anyone is listening, the universe is, so I was sending a message." *You couldn't have done any better than that, Avery? That was so lame.*

"Nonsense! I'll only say this once more—any more crazy behaviour, and you're out. Understood? I don't want the whole village talking about you. They're all going to think I'm ridiculous for giving you lodgings."

"Ah, I don't think anyone would think that. Maybe they'd think you're a kind and wonderful person?" Hmm, it would take a lot for that to happen. Thankfully, Adam was keeping to himself and waiting for me to be done. Two arguments at once were too much for me to handle.

She folded her arms. "They know I'm not kind or wonderful. This is your last warning." She jutted her chin out for good measure, then spun around and went back inside.

When I turned back to Adam, he was laughing. I narrowed my eyes at him and growled, "Shut it," in the lowest, quietest voice I could. "Come on." Without explaining, I went to my car and unlocked it. I looked around to make sure no one was watching. "I need to ask you some questions. I'm allowing you into my car, but act like a jerk, or try and hurt me, and I'll banish you without a second thought. Understood?"

A flicker of dread passed through his eyes. Hmm, I knew he didn't like it, but being scared? Looked like I had more power in this situation than I'd thought. He pursed his lips. "Fine."

I got in. He was already seated in the passenger seat. He looked at me. "I hope this means you're getting closer to discovering who killed me."

"Possibly." Well, I couldn't be getting further away, so it wasn't a lie.

He folded his arms, all the aggro energy of before gone. "Ask away."

I pulled my phone out of my bag so it looked like I was talking to someone. Why I didn't think of that earlier, I had no idea. Oh, yeah, probably because I was freaking out. Anyway…. "First cab off the rank. There was a man at the club chatting with Coach Atherton. They were talking about your demise having come at the right time for the club." I described the slim, forty-something guy with the shaved head and scar above his top lip.

Adam gasped, then swore. What fruity language he had. Super inventive. When he was done with that, he tried to pound his fist onto my dash, but it sliced through. At least he wasn't in poltergeist mode. Could they be strong enough to ruin dashboards? Imagine trying to explain that to the insurance company. Yep, no payout for you. "Those turds. I can't believe Coach would say that." His eyes focussed on me, and I suppressed a shudder at the threat in them. "Are you lying? Are you trying to turn me against my friends?"

I rolled my eyes. "Of course not. Why would I do that? I'm trying to help. To be honest, I want you gone sooner rather than later, and if I solve this, you'll leave me alone. You might even get to go to the next place. Who knows?" I didn't mention that it was probably hell. The last thing I wanted was for him to stop me solving this.

"Yeah, well, that can't come soon enough. I want to date some hot babes." I was dealing with a complete idiot. I wasn't sure what went on in the afterlife, but why would it be so similar to here? What was the point of living and dying if the next place was identical? I mean, maybe it was, but that didn't make sense to my small brain. Could he be smarter than me? He tried to adjust the seat, but his hand went straight through. Hmm, nope, not smarter than me.

"Right, okay. Best get this done quickly then. So, who was that man, and why would he be happy about you dying?"

He stared out the windscreen. "I don't know if I should tell you. Maybe you'll hate me and won't help me any more."

I smiled. "There's no risk of me hating you any more than I already do. Honestly. I promise I'll keep investigating until I unravel this mystery."

Surprisingly, he chuckled. "I never thought I'd be happy for a woman to say that to me, but there you go." His Adam's apple bobbed as he swallowed. "Right, so that's the club's solicitor, Oliver Brown." He scratched the back of his neck. "Before I died, there was a small drama. Coach didn't like something that happened." With this guy, it could be anything. I stared at him while he mustered the courage to tell me what it was. "A week before I was killed, two women went to a solicitor, and their solicitor went to Coach. The women threatened to go to the police and have me arrested."

He was taking forever to get to it, so I helped him along. "What did you do? Did you rape them?" That was the first thing that came to mind.

His spine jerked straight, and his gaze jumped to mine. "No. I had sex with them. They never said no. They just wanted money. Their solicitor told Coach if I settled, they would sign something and promise never to go to the police. Coach believed me, but he said I had to keep a low profile until he could get it sorted."

Now we were getting somewhere. Had the coach killed him to make this all go away? There was more to it for sure. After the experience I'd just had, maybe I knew what it was. "What were their names?"

He shrugged. "Maggie and Pam."

"Just Maggie and Pam?"

"How am I supposed to know their last names? Coach mentioned them, but I wasn't really listening."

For goodness' sake. What a poo smear this guy was. If he got shown the bright light when it was his turn, I was going to scream. "And where did you meet them?"

"At a club. Met lots of babes there. Clubs are great pickup spots. You know, women are mad for rugby players, and once they've got a few drinks into them, they're only too happy to go home."

And here we were getting to the crux of it. "Did you maybe slip drugs into their drinks to make sure they were compliant?"

"It wasn't to make them more compliant. I just like what I like."

Vomit snaked up my throat. I swallowed it down. I was glad he was dead, and I betted those women were too. "Hang on a moment." I got out of the car and breathed in clear air. If that black hole didn't open for him when he was going to the other side, I'd open it myself. Pushing my anger and disgust to the side, I slid back into the car. Bellamy needed me to figure it out. I wasn't going to let him down. "So you drugging and raping these women are what they were trying to cover up?"

"Yeah. I s'pose so."

"Where did you get the drugs from?"

"I don't wanna get a brother into trouble."

"Was it Joel?"

His eyes widened. "How'd you know?"

"Lucky guess." I rubbed my temples, took my notebook out of my bag, and wrote it all down. "Did Coach Atherton know it was him?"

"No. I wasn't gonna tell."

"Why didn't the coach just fire you?"

He smirked. "My uncle pretty much funds that club. He couldn't."

I kept a straight face, but I wanted to smile. "So, the fact that he couldn't fire you might be what got you killed."

His forehead wrinkled. "What?" He thought about it for a bit, and it was a beautiful moment when understanding dawned. "No way. He wouldn't have. After that lecture he gave me about breaking the law, I doubt he would risk it. He has a wife and three kids. He was always going on about how he loves his life."

"Do you think Cath could've done it?"

"Nah, man. She loved me."

"But she knew you cheated."

"Not until afterwards."

Time for a home truth. "Well, she certainly moved on quickly."

He frowned. "You're lying. There's no way."

"You don't have to believe me, but do you want to see the pics?" I pulled my phone out and brought up Xavier's Instagram. There was a selfie of him, and in the background, Cath and Dave joined at the lips. "So, that's not Cath and Dave?"

He tried to grab the phone and failed. My hand froze, but it was a small price to pay to see the look of pure shock on his face. Irritation followed it. He swore and called her a few names. "How could she?"

"How could you? You cheated on her for most, if not all, of your relationship." I couldn't believe I had to point out the obvious. Actually, I could believe it. This was Adam I was dealing with.

"But I'm famous. I'm a guy. It's not the same."

I didn't have the time or energy to try and convince a ghost he was wrong. He'd never change. His beliefs were his problem and no one else's now he was dead. "Who's more likely to have killed you?

Cath, Coach, Dave, or Xavier? Or is there someone else I don't know about who hated you?" I didn't like including Xavier. He was such a lovely guy, and I just didn't get those vibes from him. Not that killers couldn't be good actors or clever. But my sixth sense told me it wasn't him.

"There's no one else I can think of. Everyone loved me. Me and the team, we were one big happy family." His opinion was likely to be because he was oblivious about how much he upset other people. "I can't believe Coach would have either. Out of all of them, Cath would be my bet. She always had a jealous streak. Or maybe Dave since he's with her now." This guy was doing my head in. "Have they replaced me yet?" He didn't sound too happy about the prospect.

"Kind of. Byron's in the team." Wow, how had I remembered that? I was surprised something came back to me from the other night. Maybe I wasn't all the way out of it when he told me?

Adam laughed and laughed and laughed. "Oh, that's a good one. Pull the other leg."

"I'm pretty sure that's what he said, but I guess I could be wrong." Maybe I'd hallucinated it? No. No I was sure he said it. But did I really know? Most of that night shortly after going upstairs was a blur. I couldn't be sure.

"Of course you're wrong. That kid's too green. He has potential, but he's not nearly ready. He was keen, of course, and the coach was thinking of giving him a go, but as captain, I had a say, and we would've had to cut Xavier, and he was much better, even though he's gay." And there it was—another reminder of how gross this man was. As much as I never wanted to die, at least there was death to get rid of people like Adam. It was sad that nice people had to leave the earth, too, but life, as we all knew, wasn't perfect. Neither was death. Yikes, this ghost was turning me into a macabre person. Another incentive to get this thing solved ASAP.

"Just to be clear, you're sure the coach wouldn't have done it? It would save him a lot of problems. I would imagine if that news got out, all the money in the world wouldn't have made him keep you on the team, and if he was found to have turned a blind eye, he might get in trouble too." I had no idea how far the cover up went, but maybe the coach knew this stuff was going on. Maybe he'd been at nightclubs with them when they'd left with the women. Things like this were rarely isolated incidents. I wasn't sure the club condoned this behaviour, but they certainly didn't police their players. Joel was a prime example.

"Well, we did have a couple of salty arguments before I was killed, so even though I doubt it, it's possible. I was his star player though."

Was it possible we were getting somewhere? I was going to see Bellamy straight after this. I had a feeling we were getting close. "Yes, but he was potentially going to lose you anyway, and the whole team's rep would've taken a beating. Imagine trying to get funding after that. Who's going to sponsor a team that has players who do what you and Joel did?"

He stared at me but said nothing. "I guess that's for you to work out."

"Right." So helpful. "Did you and Dave get along?" Time to change tack.

His gaze moved to the windscreen. Lie incoming. "Yeah, sure. Of course."

"Why is he disrespecting you so soon after you died? Whether Cath started with him before or after you died, don't you think he should've waited before being obvious about it?" Poke, poke, poke. My gut told me he still wasn't giving me the full story about everything.

He looked at me this time. "Of course he should. He was always too big for his boots. He was jealous of me being captain over him." Wow, seemed like everyone was jealous of him or because of him. He didn't get that he was the common denominator in all of these bad relationships.

"Which means he could've killed you without any urging from Cath? I don't think so. And I don't buy that Cath talked him into it. If she didn't start dating him till after you died, then there isn't enough loyalty there yet. What else would his motivation be? You think he could've killed you, but why? Tell the truth. I don't get why you won't be totally truthful with me."

"I told you before—I want you to help me, and I know how uppity and judgemental you are. You hate that men can have fun and walk away from a woman. You're like every woman I've ever known." He lifted his chin as if he'd just taken the higher ground.

I gave him a withering look. "You're ignorant and stupid." His eye twitched. "I don't care about who you are or what you did any more. I just want to get to the truth and figure this out. Please just cut the bull and spill it. If you won't tell me everything, I can't help you, and I'm done." I put my hand on the door as if I was about to open it and leave.

He leaned over and tried to grab my wrist. As his ghost fingers slid through my arm, I shuddered at the stab of ice. He swore. I didn't think I'd heard the F-word so much in such a short period of time. "Damn this stupid existence!"

I ignored his temper tantrum. "Well? Are you going to tell me, or am I leaving?"

"I slept with his sister a few times. She thought we were dating, and when I told her I was seeing other people, she lost it. That night, I slept with her again, but she didn't want to. Dave found out because she ratted me out. He threatened me. Said if I ever went near his sister again, he'd kill me." This guy was the pits. Whoever had killed him had saved many women much pain.

The suspects with enough motive to do this were adding up. Should I be putting Dave's sister on the list? I grabbed the steering wheel and lowered my head to rest it on my forearms. This was a nightmare. The more I shone a light on Adam's past, the more suspects appeared. "Is there anything else you need to tell me? Any other threats? Any other women you've attacked? Please tell me now."

He thought about it. "No one else. Well, no one who threatened me. Do you think you have enough information? Who do you think it was?"

"At this point, I'm not sure, but the standout is Dave." But was it? I cast my mind back to when Cath was crying about Adam having cheated on her. It seemed as if she really had just found out the week before he died, and she wasn't aggro. She was sad. Maybe dating Dave made her feel better, or maybe he was genuinely a great guy? Did she play with knives? Yes. Did she kill him? I sighed. I didn't know. It was time to talk to Bellamy. "I have more work to do, but I'll let you know tonight or tomorrow. Is that okay?"

"Yeah, fine. I'll be waiting at your fence."

"Can you not? Mrs Crabby's giving me a hard time, and I don't need to give her any excuses to get rid of me. Just wait next to my car."

"It's all the same to me."

"Right. I'll see you later." As I slid out of the car, he was still sitting there. The idea of him waiting in my car creeped me out. I knew I'd invited him in, but could I uninvite him? From what everyone had said—ghosts and humans alike—getting a ghost out of your space was way harder than asking them to visit. I wasn't about to call a priest to exorcise my car. "Can you get out, please?"

He looked at me forlornly, but I wasn't buying it. "Do I have to?"

"Yes. Get out of my car now." Just like that, he disappeared. Imagine that—he listened to me. Miracles would never cease. I kept my crystal in my hand because it would be just like him to come back and surprise me for fun. Before I locked the car, I called Bellamy.

"Winters. Good to hear from you. Have you got something?"

"I have many somethings, but I don't know if it narrows things down or makes everything worse. In any case, I can come see you now if you're around."

"Indeed, I am. See you soon." The line closed. I must be getting used to people not saying goodbye because it didn't bother me this time. Go me.

I jumped back in my car and headed over. For once, I was happy that I hadn't told Finnegan about me helping Bellamy. This way, he wouldn't be able to put two and two together. Some of the things I was going to tell the sergeant about, I was going to put down to hearing things last night. He didn't know I'd been drugged, so he wouldn't think it strange I could remember so much. As for any information I couldn't put down to that, well, I was going to just say that I had my methods. He might need proof of some things before he'd act, but it would likely be easy to find out. With the information about the women being attacked, well, he could easily call in the coach and grill him until he caved. He might lawyer up, but Bellamy could threaten to leak it to the papers. I had the women's first names. That might freak the coach out enough to talk. Bellamy could bluff and say he'd spoken to the women.

Dave would be an easy one—I could say a few players had told me but wanted to remain anonymous. An interview with Dave's sister would at least give motive. Dave threatening Adam would be a case of hearsay, unfortunately. But it would be an incentive for Bellamy to revisit interviewing the player.

When I walked into the station, the PC at the front desk sent me straight through. It was a great feeling to be on the "inside." Knowing I wasn't going to be turned away meant I walked in there relaxed and happy. Silly me. I should've known.

I knocked on Bellamy's door.

"Come in." That tone was harsher than I remembered. Had I caught him at a bad time? I opened the door and entered. His frowny face greeted me. "Sit." He pointed at the seat. Yep, he was wearing a police uniform, and Sergeant Fox stood behind his chair. He was also giving me the "disappointed father" look.

I sat. "Nice to see you too." I figured I had nothing left to lose. I might as well put on a brave front. Had someone told him about Saturday night? I wasn't game to ask and accidentally dob myself in, so I waited.

He didn't make me wait long for the answer.

"I heard what happened on Saturday night, and I'm appalled you didn't report it to the police. What were you thinking? If no one reports these things, we can't do anything about it. You've probably endangered other women not speaking up. What do you have to say for yourself?"

My mouth opened, ready to argue, but I knew he was right. It was also difficult to think of what to say because Fox was giving me a piece of his mind too. "He's right. What were you thinking? And why didn't you come and tell me? This is unacceptable."

"I didn't want any dramas while we're trying to figure out this case. We can deal with it later. Who told you?" I was probably asking a redundant question. It must have been—

"Finnegan, of course. That lad's got more sense than you, which surprises me more than you can imagine. He was very worried. He called me from the hospital that night."

Argh, tattletale. And why didn't he mention anything when I asked him not to tell the police yet? Come to think of it, he had looked a bit cagey at breakfast. Hmm. I was going to have to have words. But they would be gentle ones. I'd probably do the same if it had happened to a friend. Why did I think I didn't deserve anyone's help? Now wasn't the time to go down that road. "He's a good guy, Sergeant. Can I be honest?"

"It's about time."

I smiled. He didn't even know how many lies I'd told, and that included lies by omission. If he saw who I really was, the only time he'd let me back in here was to put me in a cell. Lying for survival didn't make me an evil person, just not a great person. And this time, I'd wanted to keep it quiet because I was selfish. Yep, if everyone thought I was kind, they were mistaken. If you looked at who my parents were, of course I wasn't going to be the best person in the universe. "I was afraid if you knew I'd gotten myself in trouble, you would never ask me to help you again. I'm passionate about my job, and I love being able to help you. Investigating cases is enjoyable, and I love the extra insight I get, which makes my job easier. So, yes, I was being selfish. I have no other defence. Sorry if I've disappointed you." And that was it. Nothing more to add.

He cleared his throat. "Well, okay then. Are you sure you're all right?"

What, no more lecture? That was unexpected. "I'm fine. I have a bit of memory loss, and I'm obviously unhappy about what someone did, but I'm physically unharmed."

"If you need any counselling, let me know. Because it happened while you were on the job for me, I can get you access to our counsellors. They're very good." He picked up his stapler and clicked it a few times.

"That's wonderfully kind of you, Sergeant. Thank you. If I need the help, I'll let you know. Your offer is appreciated." Wow, two surprises in one meeting. Looked like his bark was worse than his bite. He could've gone on and on, but instead, he offered help. The clicking of the stapler was awkward in the silence, so I put us both out of our misery and spoke. "Would you like to know what I've found out? As well as talking to a few people on Saturday night, I've been stalking the players' social media."

He placed the stapler on the table and looked at me. "Please, go on."

"Remember I told you about the man I'd overheard the coach talking to on Saturday?" He nodded. "Well, I've found out who he is. He's the team lawyer, Oliver Brown, and you're going to love what else I found out." I told him what Adam said about the women. "The coach was in a Catch-22 situation. Fire Adam and get the women off their back but lose funding from the mayor, or keep Adam and give the club a bad name, plus risk losing future funding and supporters. It sounds like a lose-lose proposition."

He scratched the back of his head as he thought. While he did that, Fox spoke. "How did you find that out? I didn't tell you any of that."

"I know. I bit the bullet and spoke to Adam this morning. I got it out of him." I gasped. *Idiot.*

"What did you say?" Bellamy's eyes were wide.

Fox mouthed, "I'm sorry." I ignored him, finally.

"Ah, I don't know. I kind of blanked for a bit. Maybe it's trauma from Saturday night? I was having all these weird dreams, and I think some of it was from people talking to me or me overhearing stuff, but my thoughts from that night still get a bit jumbled." Argh, now he was going to question any information I passed on about Saturday night. *Damn you for losing your sense of where you were, Avery.* It was bound to happen eventually. At least I kind of had an excuse for the nutty outburst. "So, what do you think about the coach being a suspect?"

"I think it's worth investigating further. You've done some good work, Winters. Anything else to report?" Thank goodness he was as willing to gloss over my craziness as I was. I told him about Dave's sister. "Who told you that?"

"They want to remain anonymous. Dave and Cath, Adam's ex, are together now as well. They were all over each other at the club. Which is something I remember, but I also found pics on the net." I brought up the pictures on my phone that I'd screenshotted. "Here." I handed him my phone. "They're in the background of that one and the next one."

"They're... cosy."

"Very. The other thing my source told me is that Dave might have wanted the captaincy of the team, but Adam was standing in his way. I can't give you proof, though. Maybe you could question the coach about that one?" He'd likely be honest if it was a thing. Lumping suspicion onto someone else sounded like a good defence strategy.

He handed my phone back. "We know Cath is proficient with knives, but the knife that was used is a different type and weight to what she uses for throwing. There was no DNA evidence linking her to it either. We only got the report back this morning. I thought I'd let you know. But can you email me those pictures of Dave and Cath anyway, and a link to where you got them from?"

"Sure thing." So Cath was sort of in the clear. She still might have instructed Dave to do it. If only we had more concrete evidence.

"Have you got anything else? Are you ready to report the drink spiking?"

He snuck that one in. "Well, they won't have the lab results back for a few days, so I figured I'd wait until they were sure. My suspicion is obviously that Joel did it. He's the one who was going to benefit. And it's likely not the first time. If Adam was doing nefarious things like that, he might have had a partner in crime."

"Good point. We'll chase up that angle, too, at least as far as getting whoever did this held accountable. I hate to say it, but because nothing else happened, if we can even prove who did this, they'll just get a slap on the wrist. Proving it without video evidence will be near impossible." He gave me an apologetic look.

I started laughing. Before I knew it, I was doubled over, and tears were gushing down my face. Seriously, he got upset I didn't tell him, and when I did, he admitted it was a waste of time. When I finally settled down enough to talk, I said, "This is another reason I didn't bother telling you. It's going to make little to no difference. No offence."

He raised an eyebrow. "None taken. Let me assure you, though, this is just as frustrating for us as it is for you. The laws don't always support us in our job, unfortunately. But it is what it is, and we do our best."

"I know, and I appreciate it." Time to try my luck. "Will your officers go back to the rugby club to do any interviews?"

"Yes, why?"

"Do you think I could tag along? The coach kicks me out every time, but I'd like to be there to get a feel for what's going down and to take some photos. When this is solved, it'll be good for my article to have as much information as possible."

"I don't see why not. I'll message you when I know the time. I'll look at getting this done today, provided the coach is there."

"Okay. Chat soon." I stood. Some of the weight pressing on my shoulders lifted. The meeting had gone well, all things considered. I'd almost created a disaster by talking to Fox. It was a good reminder to check myself more often. If only I could tell people. Not that I was keen to before, but after Finnegan told me what happened to his sister and that scammer using the fact that she could supposedly talk to dead people as her angle, and his hatred of that, there was no way in Hades I was ever going to tell him or anyone around here. Which made my life hard but not impossible. It would be worse if Finnegan hated me. I didn't think I could handle that. So shouldering my ghostly burden on my own was the only choice.

As I walked out the door, Fox said, "Thank you, Avery. And be careful." As much as I appreciated his words, I wasn't going to respond. I'd flown close to the sun today and gotten away with it.

But I was going to be smarter than Icarus because I didn't want to crash and burn, or was that burn and crash? The door clicked shut behind me. Even though I thought I'd gotten away with it, a niggling feeling told me that I hadn't or wouldn't.

Was I about to do an Icarus, and I didn't even know it?

CHAPTER 19

I was just finishing lunch with Meg when my phone rang. "Hello, Sergeant. Have you got a time?"

"We're going now, and I'd suggest you get there quickly. This might not take long. After our conversation, we did some more digging and discovered that Coach Atherton's alibi for the morning of the murder doesn't add up. The person decided they didn't want to lie for him any more, so we're going to bring him to the station for questioning. See you at the club ASAP."

When he hung up, my mouth was still open and catching flies.

"What is it, Aves?" Meg's concerned face snapped me out of my shock.

"There's been a massive development in Adam's murder investigation. I have to get my bum over to the rugby fields to meet the police." I stood and grabbed my bag.

Meg stood too. "I'd say be careful, but if the police are going to be there, you should be good. Honestly, after the other night, Bails and I are worried you're going to get yourself into something you can't get out of. We want to shadow you everywhere." She gave me a cheesy grin and hugged me. "You're important to us, just in case you didn't realise."

I tightened my hug and pretended my voice wasn't shaky with emotion. "Thank you. And you guys are important to me too. Thank you for always being there for me."

"Ditto." She stepped back and smiled. "Go get that story."

I grinned. "I'll let you know what happens later."

"Please do."

When Bailey realised I was leaving, he came out from behind the bar—it had unfortunately been too busy for him to join us for lunch—and gave me a hug too. Boy, did it feel good to be enclosed in his strong arms. He was rather cuddly. A girl could get used to this. But she wasn't going to. "Take care, okay."

"I will. Promise."

When the hug was over, I hurried out. I didn't want to look into his eyes after the other night when I proclaimed my love for him. Some embarrassing things took longer to get over than others.

Excitement bubbled in my stomach on the way to the rugby club. I didn't want to get ahead of myself, but it would be so awesome if the case was solved. Knowing it was because of my information made it so much sweeter. Not being able to tell Bellamy about the trophy stabbed in his eye had been frustrating, but at least their investigations had centred on the club and not another area of his life. I imagined the police had been trying to find what had caused that eye wound. Bellamy had never told me about it, but if their coroner wasn't totally useless, it wouldn't escape their notice. It was pretty obvious. Maybe they'd discover the trophy for themselves after searching the coach's home or office? I tried not to worry about the fact that they might have been able to solve things more quickly if they'd known about the trophy.

When I turned up, the police weren't there. My nervous energy wouldn't let me sit in the car, so I hopped out and walked to the entry gate. Oh, that was interesting. It looked like a reporter and TV crew were there. What was going on? Surely no one else had gotten the scoop on the breaking story. I'd be mightily disappointed if Bellamy had tipped off another news team about this. Nah, he wouldn't undermine his mate's son's place of work either, would he? Unless another officer had done it.

Wary of being kicked out again, I walked into the gate and closer to the action, but I stopped at a distance. The camera guy had his camera pointed towards the club. Three men had their backs to me—it looked like Coach Atherton, Byron, and Dave. Hmm, interesting. This must be about something else. Unfortunately, these media people were going to get in on the other action. As much as it irked me, at least they didn't know the full story.

Because Coach Atherton was occupied by the reporter with the microphone and there was media here, he would be unlikely to either notice me or kick me out. *You got this, Avery.* Despite my nervousness, I approached the group and stood so I could see and hear everything, but I was off to the side.

The reporter was one I recognised from nightly sports reports on ITV. Owen Kowalski moved the microphone towards Dave, who was holding a medium-sized trophy of a rugby player running, the ball safely tucked under one arm. "How does it feel to be announced captain of the team? You've got some big shoes to fill." It was at that moment that the coach realised I was there. He frowned, but I was right—he didn't say anything. Now wasn't the time to make a commotion. Thank Hades.

My attention focussed back on Dave. He smiled at Owen, and I recorded with my phone. Not that I could use this, but information gathering was my thing. "Adam was an incredible player and leader, and I'm not trying to fill his shoes. I'll do things differently for sure, but hopefully, I'll be strong enough to keep the team winning." Hmm, so Adam dying had resulted in a lot of things changing for the better for Dave. Argh! I hated that I wasn't sure. And Bellamy was about to come here and arrest the coach.

Owen asked, "Is that your trophy from last season's final win?"

Dave held it up. "Yes. Everyone on the team has one just like it. I brought it because it reminds me how great we were and that I need to stay focussed so the team can get another fantastic result. I don't want all of Adam's work to be in vain."

"I'm sure you'll do great. If Coach Atherton believes in you, then you must be right for the job." Owen smiled and turned to

Byron. "So, congratulations on being the new recruit. How are you feeling?"

Byron grinned. "Tip-top. I can't believe I've finally got an opportunity to play with these guys. I've looked up to them for years, and to be amongst them on the field, well, it's a dream come true. And I have Coach Atherton to thank." He turned to the coach. "Thank you for believing in me."

The coach smiled. "You have real talent. It's just been a shame that it's taken something so tragic to get you there, but what's done is done, and we, as a team, have to move on. I'm sure Adam would be so proud of you."

Byron's smile wavered but then reasserted itself. Hmm, he must know that the coach was feeding him a line of bulldust. Did Byron know how much a part Adam had played in him not getting a spot on the team?

The reporter pointed to Byron's smaller trophy of a rugby player holding a ball aloft. It was about half the size of Dave's. "And what's that trophy for?"

Byron looked at the trophy. "It's to remind me where I came from and what I can achieve. I got this last year for service to the club. It was a real honour to be so appreciated." There was something I wasn't getting. *Come on, brain. Tell me what it is.*

Movement caught the corner of my eye. I turned towards the entry gate. Bellamy strode through it, five officers behind him. The reporter noticed and indicated his cameraman should film. Furrows inserted themselves into Atherton's forehead, and he turned, as did Byron and Dave.

I kept filming.

Bellamy reached us. His officers circled Atherton. One of the policemen I recognised stood directly in front of Atherton and said, "I'm PC Patel. You're under arrest on suspicion of murdering Adam Murphy. You do not have to say anything. But, it may harm your defence if you do not mention when questioned something which you later rely on in court. Anything you do say may be given in evidence. Please turn around."

Atherton paled. He glanced at Owen. "If you put this on the news, I'll sue you, and you'll never get access to this club again."

Owen turned to his camera guy and made a slicing-neck motion for cut it. The cameraman lowered his equipment.

"Please turn around." Patel stood, cuffs ready.

"What is this? You can't be serious? I would never murder anyone, let alone my star player."

Bellamy stared at him. "Would you like to do this here? I can lay it all out for everyone to hear if you're game."

"You'll hear from my solicitor. You have no reason to arrest me." He turned and placed his hands behind his back. Patel cuffed him. As they led him away, Bellamy gave me a look, turned, and left. Owen and his team followed, leaving Dave, Byron, and me on the grass.

I watched them leave, not sure how I felt. Something was still wrong, but I wasn't sure what. What had I missed?

Dave looked at me. "Coach did it? Seriously? I don't believe that." He shook his head. "This is all absolute bull crap. My one moment and Adam still manages to ruin it. Even dead, he's a pain in my arse." Dave stomped off towards the parking lot.

"Wow, that was... a lot." Byron gave a wry grin. "I wonder if they'll show any of that."

"I doubt it. Unless they want to be sued."

"Oh, I don't mean about Coach's arrest. I meant about me making the team and Dave making captain. We both earned it, and we deserve our moment in the sun. Adam was always taking all the credit for everything." He glared at his trophy. "I almost had a proper trophy... like Dave's. I would've been on the team last year if it wasn't for Adam." He looked at me, but it was as if he was looking through me. "Adam thought I didn't know he convinced Coach to leave me out. But I know everything that goes on around here. The hundreds of hours I've spent handing out water bottles, lugging equipment, even picking up their damn pizza, calling them Ubers, calling Coach when nights out got out of hand. You name it, I've done it. And for all that, I got this pathetic trophy and the nickname Lappy, as in lapdog. The crap Adam put me through. He came up with that nickname, and some of the team still use it."

And that's when I realised it. My stomach dropped, and the moisture fled my mouth. I licked my lips. "Has anyone else ever gotten one of those?"

His eyes narrowed. "What do you mean?"

"Well, if you're the only one who's ever gotten one, it would mean they did appreciate you, that you *are* special."

The smile that appeared held a touch of evil. It was a *knowing* smile. "I am special, Avery. Did you know that not only am I good at rugby, I also have a fantastic memory?" He obviously wanted me to wonder where this conversation was going. The sensation of scratchy cockroach feet on the back of my neck made me shudder, and I took a step back. He knew I knew he was the killer. I eyed the gate to the car park that Dave had gone through a minute before, and he laughed. "You can't outrun me, Avery, and now there's no one here but us. Aren't you going to ask how I know you know?"

"Nope." Okay, I did want to know—the have-to-know-every-thing curiosity of the journalist was still alive and well within me—but I didn't want to give him the satisfaction.

"Fine. I'll tell you anyway. Joel."

Despite not wanting to buy into it, I said, "Joel?" Maybe this conversation would earn me time to figure out how in Hades I was going to get out of here with my life. I had no doubt he intended to kill me. Whether here or somewhere else, I didn't know. But unconscious people could easily be transported in car boots.

"Saturday night, after he roofied you and took you downstairs, you babbled about seeing ghosts. You told him someone stabbed Adam in the eye with a trophy. You also said you couldn't tell anyone because you'd look crazy. I was betting on that, so I did nothing. I also knew you didn't have any idea who owned the trophy. Maybe today was my mistake." He cocked his head to the side and waved said trophy around. "But in the end, it doesn't matter. I worked hard to do this club a favour and get rid of Adam. Coach didn't tell me to directly, but I knew he wanted him gone. Adam made messes, and everyone was sick of cleaning them up. And I wanted my spot on the team. Adam only did things to benefit himself. By killing him, I helped the whole team. Coach will get off because he didn't do it, and they can't prove it. So now, I have to get rid of you and this trophy. Shame, really, because I earned the damned thing."

Wow, he'd seemed like such a nice young man. Boy, was my radar off. Some things never changed.

Maybe if I screamed, someone would hear? There hadn't been anyone on the tennis courts when I'd driven in, but maybe someone was there? Maybe Peta was in the clubhouse? I knew I couldn't outrun him. The gate was too far away. And he was bigger, stronger, and fitter than me. Hapkido might work, but only if I took him by surprise, and then I would still have to run that distance to the car park. Thing was, I wasn't going to go quietly, so even though there was no perfect option, I'd have to choose one.

I sucked in a deep breath, opened my mouth wide, and screamed ear-piercingly. He leaped towards me, and I ran backwards, still screaming. If I tried to run too fast, I'd lose the air I needed for screaming. Within a few seconds, his chest was at my back, one arm looped around my front, pinning me to him, the other hand firmly over my mouth. One of my arms was trapped against my side. "Big mistake." Maybe for him it was, but not for me. The biggest mistake I could make was doing nothing. We were in an open field. People were around nearby. As long as I could manage not to get knocked out in the next few minutes, I had a good chance of survival.

Also, Bellamy was going to kill me when he found out I'd steered him wrong... again. But that was a for-later problem. I still had a bigger one to solve.

He started dragging me towards the clubhouse. "There's no one in there. No one is coming to save you either, so you may as well give up."

No chance in Hades of that, buster.

He was even stronger than he looked. Not that I was heavy, but I weighed around sixty-five kilos. That wasn't nothing. My feet weren't even touching the ground, and his hand was pressed so hard against my open mouth that I couldn't even bite him. This sucked. And I didn't want to die. Sure, I loved my ghost friends, but I wasn't ready to join them.

How was I going to get out of this? Should I try something else or wait for the right opportunity? Waiting would be best, but what if nothing good came? Stop. Of course it would come. It had to. But did it? People were killed all the time. Their chance for it to stop never came.

We were almost at the clubhouse door.

Nausea swelled in my chest. It travelled up my throat but had nowhere to go because Byron's hand was jammed against my mouth. Oh, Hades, I was going to die by choking on my own vomit, and he'd never even go to gaol for that. Why me?

The tidal wave of nausea exploded through my open mouth into his hand. "What the? Is that what I think it is?" As I started to choke, he dropped me. "You're disgusting."

I vomited all over the ground. Byron started dry retching. Even though I wasn't sure I'd finished, I made a break for it and spoke to Siri. "Hey, Siri, call Bellamy."

I put my phone in my skirt pocket—yay for denim skirts—microphone side up, so maybe Byron wouldn't notice it until I'd warned the sergeant. I'd made it halfway to the gate and freedom. Byron's heavy footsteps sounded on the ground behind me. I wasn't sure if Bellamy had answered, but I spoke anyway. It was the only chance I might have. "Help! Come back to the rugby club. Byron did it. Byron killed Adam. He's trying to k—"

A heavy body slammed into me from behind.

I slammed to the ground, the wind knocked out of me. Pain exploded in my chest and back. I tried to breathe in, but it wouldn't come. Winded.

Byron grabbed my ponytail and got off me. I was able to suck in air, finally. "Nice try, Avery, but no deal." He pulled me towards the clubhouse. I didn't have the energy to scream, but my hands were free, and I grabbed my phone. The call was still live! He had answered it. I screamed, "Help! Rugby club. Help!"

Byron yanked my hair again, jerking me around to face him.

"What's this?" He snatched my phone, took one look at it, and dropped it at his feet, then stomped on it with his heel. The glass cracked, and the screen went black.

"Game's over. The police heard everything."

It was his turn to scream. Rage erupted from his mouth. His head jerked around as he looked down the field, then towards the gate and back at the clubhouse. He glared at me with cold eyes. "Without you, they have nothing. If you're missing, they won't be able to prove I killed you."

"You've gone mad. They're going to come for you. Of course they'll know. Give up now, Byron." Maybe *I'd* gone mad. Saying this stuff would likely aggravate him, not convince him to leave me alone. "You'll do more time if you kill me. Just stop now. Maybe I can convince them I was mucking around? As you said, they don't know about the trophy. I don't want to die. I promise not to say anything. Besides, I can't tell them how I know, and they'll likely ignore me. Who am I, anyway? I'm a nobody. They won't listen to me." Argh, I hated begging. I hated that he felt power in this moment, even though, ultimately, he was going to be arrested. At least, I hoped so.

His vacant eyes warned me just in time. He grabbed my wrist with one iron hand and raised the trophy with the other. Hades! He was going to stab me with the trophy.

My heart raced, and I focussed. I acted without conscious thought as my training kicked in. I didn't have time to wonder if it would work, and I had no choice anyway. This was it.

I jerked my hand towards me, freeing my wrist from his grip. Then I dropped low. Kicking my leg out and spinning fast at the same time, I swept his legs out from under him.

And I ran.

This time I reached the gate. I didn't know if it was wishful thinking, but I swore sirens were coming. Too faint. How far away were they?

I risked a quick look behind.

Byron was after me.

I gulped in breath after breath as I sprinted past my car. There

DIONNE LISTER

was no way I'd have time to find my keys, unlock it, and jump in with him after me. If I could make it far enough, either the police would be here, or I'd find someone, anyone. I wanted to scream, but I didn't have the capacity.

The gravel was loose under my shoes, and I almost slipped. If he tackled me here, it would hurt. And if he was adamant he wanted me dead, he could stab me there and then and be done with it.

Hades.

I didn't know it was possible, but I moved my legs faster, muscles on fire with the effort. The sound of his speedy footfalls behind me reverberated in my ears. But there was an even louder sound.

Sirens.

I didn't stop, though. He'd lost all semblance of sanity. Did he even care that the police were near?

He was right behind me, within tackling distance. I sensed him diving. I launched to the side. This was going to hurt, but at least it wouldn't kill me. The back of one hand hit first as I curved it. I managed a half cat roll, half side roll, the ground gouging my arm as I rolled, the unforgiving surface stabbing my back and shoulders as I completed the roll and leaped to my feet in one smooth motion. I gave thanks to my instructor, who'd made us do those rolls on concrete over and over to make sure we knew what bits not to slam on the ground.

I heaved in breath after breath. Could I stand here and give my lungs a break? My leg muscles were fatigued, and my throat was raw from screaming and breathing too hard. Nope, no rest for me. Byron was like the Terminator.

He scrambled to his feet, knees and hands bleeding, but his robotic face revealed no hint of pain. Where had that nice young man from Saturday night gone? Had Adam's treatment driven him crazy, or was he already like that?

Holding the trophy overhead in a ready-to-strike position, he advanced. I didn't dare turn my back, so I walked backwards. I was too spent to outrun him. He trained for this; I didn't.

The peal of sirens had been getting louder, and I hadn't noticed.

They were hitting a crescendo. Dared I hope I was going to be okay?

Byron catapulted himself towards me as tyres skidded in the gravel behind me. He could still land a killing blow. I tried to dodge to my right. But he grabbed my left arm as he landed.

"Drop the weapon. Freeze!"

He did none of that.

English police didn't carry guns, so Byron had time to finish what he'd started.

His pupils swallowed his irises. Black eyes locked on mine, and his arm came down.

I grabbed the arm that was gripping mine with my other hand. Moving in tandem with his forward momentum, I jerked downwards with all my force and landed on my backside. Off balance, he tripped and flew forward and down. I cringed, made myself into as small a ball as I could, and covered my head.

This was going to hurt.

But it wouldn't kill me.

He landed half on my back and half on the driveway. I couldn't see anything because he was squashing me, but there was no stabbing, so I assumed the trophy had missed, which was the plan.

And then I was being jostled. Byron's weight lifted off me, and I rolled over and jumped up, just in case. But I could relax... well, not relax, but you know... because the police had him pinned on the ground. Bellamy had one hand on the back of Byron's head, smooshing his face into the gravel, while PC Patel had his knee in his back. Another officer knelt on the ground and had a good grip on Byron's arm. He wasn't going anywhere.

When the cuffs clicked into place, my legs turned to jelly, and it was all I could do to stay standing. Adrenaline comedown commence.

Patel and the other officer wrenched Byron to his feet, and Bellamy stepped away. As his officers took him to the car, Bellamy approached me. "What did I say?"

I gave him a shaky smile. My voice wasn't much better as I fought unwanted tears. "To be careful?" I shrugged. "I tried."

He chuckled. "You call this trying?" He shook his head. "What am I going to do with you? Every time I turn around, you're in the thick of it. Am I going to have to put a protective detail on you? We don't really have the funds."

I knew he was joking, but it wouldn't be such a bad idea. "I'm sorry about getting it wrong. I really thought it might be the coach, but turns out it wasn't." I turned and looked towards the clubhouse. My phone had likely been recording the whole time until it got smashed because I never stopped it. The recording would make sure he went away for the murder, but it would out me as a woo-woo person. I wasn't ready for that yet.

"We all did. The evidence was compelling. We haven't had a chance to talk to him about why he needed someone to lie about where he was, but now that we have Byron, once we get our evidence, Atherton can go free. In fact, his solicitor is already on the phone, threatening to sue. We'll likely let him out in the morning, unless he comes clean about his alibi tonight."

"Byron stabbed Adam in the eye with that statue. You might find evidence on it."

His eyes widened. "What?! How do you know? We never released the fact that he was stabbed in the eye."

"He bragged to me before saying he was going to kill me. So you might find your case runs smoothly. He was angry that Adam talked the coach into not letting him play. I'm sure the coach will corroborate that." The police never had to know I'd recorded everything. They'd seen firsthand what he'd done to me, so I was covered. Now it was Byron's word against mine. Lucky I was such a good liar. Oh, and the little matter of Joel telling him what I'd said. That was something I'd have to deal with ASAP.

"Are you all right to drive?" The concern in his gaze was touching, but I guessed he was just doing his job. If he didn't care about the good people, why bother being a policeman?

I held my hands up. There was only a slight tremble. "I think I should be okay."

"Are you sure?"

"Yep. Positive."

"Please go straight to the station. I want to do the interview while everything is fresh in your mind. I'll have a warm cup of tea waiting for you."

I smiled. "Thanks, Sergeant. I'm looking forward to it."

"You've earned it, Winters."

I wasn't going to argue with that.

CHAPTER 20

T hree days after Byron's arrest, I was back in Bellamy's office. Guess who was in trouble again? "Why didn't you tell me those test results came back positive for Rohypnol? Do you want us to investigate?"

After the police left the rugby club, I went back and got my phone. They were sending forensics to go over the site, and I didn't want them to get it, or it would be game over for me coming across as a sane person. That night, I managed to get in touch with Joel and convince him to leave out the part of our conversation where I admitted to talking to Adam's ghost. In return, I would agree not to press charges. It was a small price to pay. We couldn't prove he drugged my drink anyway, but he didn't know that. It helped that he believed I could see ghosts, and it freaked him out. Who knew it could be a good thing?

"I've decided I don't want to press charges against anyone. I mean, how can we prove who spiked my drink? Anyone could've done it, and maybe Joel thought he was doing me a favour by getting me home safe." Okay, so his disbelieving expression told me everything I needed to know. He wasn't buying it. "Besides, I'm tired, and you have more important things to worry about. You have so much on your plate."

He blew out a loud breath. "You're not wrong there. Are you sure?"

"Positive."

"Fine. So, we've exonerated the coach. We also got phone-tower records, and we can put Byron at the supermarket at the time Adam was killed. The mayor is beyond happy that we've solved the crime, and he's promised my job is safe."

"Excellent news! I knew you could do it!"

His mouth curled up on one corner. "I? More like *we*. Thanks again for all your help. I don't know that we would've worked it out otherwise. He really didn't leave many clues. If he hadn't lost the plot at the end, he might've gotten away with it."

"Well, he didn't, so yay!" I grinned. My new phone rang. It wasn't as good as my old one because I didn't want to blow my savings, but it was better than nothing. I looked at it, then up at Bellamy. "I've been waiting for this. Is that all?"

He waved me away. "Yes, Winters. Dismissed. Until next time." A small smile broke through the deadpan look he was trying to give me.

"Thanks, Serge." I stood, then answered the phone as I walked out. "Hello, Avery Winters speaking."

"Is that Avery Winters, the journalist?"

"Yes. Who's this?" I knew who it was. I recognised her voice, and I wanted her to call. I'd set everything up that way, and she'd responded as I'd hoped she would.

"It's Adriana Oatlands. I'd like to speak to you about that article in your Letters From the Dead section. It says you wrote it."

"Well, I really just passed it on. They did sign it with a name, but they asked me not to print it yet. Why the interest?" I smirked as I exited the police station. It was fun being one step ahead of the bad guys.

"You have no idea who sent it?"

"Nope. Although it could be a friend of the murdered man. They did add a bit at the bottom, saying they would be checking in with the police, and if no one handed themselves in, they were going to send me more information. Have you been scammed too?"

She ignored my question. "What name did they sign at the bottom?"

"I promised I would keep that to myself, but for a free candle, say, a dragon, I could be bribed to show you. I'd like to come choose it though." She was desperate, and a free candle would be a small price to pay for a heads-up. Once she saw the name, she was going to run. I was going to stop that from happening. When I was done with her, she was going to march into Cranstonbury Police Station and hand herself in.

"A free candle. That's extortion."

I laughed. "A few pounds' worth of wax is extortion? I hardly think so. It's fine if you don't want to know the name. Anyway, I have to go now. B—"

"Okay, fine. You can have a dragon candle. When can you come by?"

"Right now is good for me. I'm about fifteen minutes away."

"See you soon. Goodbye."

I called Carina. "Hey, are you busy right now?"

"Not overly. Why?"

"Can you come with me to a house? I just need you to wait in the car out the front." I'd promised everyone I'd be more careful, and after the week I'd had, going to Ms Oatland's place alone was probably a dumb thing to do.

"Sure t'ing. I'm at d'e office."

"Cool. Can you pop out the front in ten?"

"Okay, Avery. Bye."

I picked Carina up and explained that I was investigating a scammer. That was enough for her to agree that she should tag along but not enough that she'd freaked out about my safety. Also, telling her she was a murderer at this point would mean me having to explain how I knew, and I couldn't.

When we arrived, I left Carina in the car with the instructions that if I wasn't out in fifteen minutes to knock on the door. Then I made my way to the front porch. I only had to knock once before

Ms Oatlands pounced on the door. Her dishevelled appearance surprised me. The article had gone in yesterday. "Hello, Ms Oatlands. Didn't get enough sleep?"

"You could say that. Please come in."

"Thanks." I walked through to the backyard, Adriana hurrying to keep up with me.

"Where are you going? For goodness' sake, you want the candle first?"

I chuckled. "Ah, no. There's just someone in your backyard that should be part of this conversation."

Her already pale complexion faded to paper white. She was more ghostly than the spirits I spoke to every day. "What are you talking about?"

"I think you know. You trapped him there."

She lifted her chin. "How dare you come into my house and spout nonsense. You don't know what you're talking about."

I was in the backyard, and I called to her husband. "Earl, are you around? It's Avery."

He appeared. "Avery, you made it! I wasn't sure if you could pull it off, but Charles assured me you were resourceful. Please, get her to free me. I can't take it any more. I feel like I'm fading away and missing my chance at going to the light. She trapped me in life, and now I'm stuck in death too." His eyes were pools of despair.

I swallowed the lump in my throat. "I'll do my best."

"Stop pretending to talk to him, dammit! Get out of my house."

I looked at her. "You wanted to know who sent me that email. No one. Your husband told me."

"You're telling me you can talk to the dead?"

I laughed. "Wow, it didn't take long. I thought it would be harder than that." She slammed a hand over her mouth about thirty seconds too late. "You buried him in your garden, then put a shed on it. You're heartless."

She shook her head. "I did no such thing."

"He told me about the scams you ran, defrauding people out of thousands of dollars. I have names and dates and amounts. I'll be going to the police with everything I know unless you go there and admit to killing him."

"Why would I do that? I didn't kill him. And you can't fool me. You can't talk to the dead."

I turned to Earl, who was staring at our exchange. "Tell me something only you would know."

"Her real name is Ethel, not Adriana, and she has webbed toes." His smile faded, the sadness that surrounded him coming back full force. "She killed me by poisoning my afternoon tea. It was tea and red velvet cake. I thought she was actually... finally being nice to me. Turns out, I was just a sucker. Her first husband died at home, suspected heart attack."

I raised a brow. "Seriously?"

"Unfortunately so."

"Stop that!" She waved her arms around, although I wasn't sure what that was going to do.

I looked at her. "Sorry, Ethel. How are those webbed toes going? From what Earl says, I should never accept meals of red velvet cake and tea from you. That was his last meal, and you fed it to him."

Her fingers came to her lips, and she swayed. "No, you can't.... No one can."

"I can, and I do every day. Earl also said that if you don't turn yourself in, he's going to ask a poltergeist he knows to make your life hell. And that poltergeist will follow you wherever you go. Even to gaol." Okay, so I made that bit up, but she wasn't to know that.

Her head shook slowly. "No. This can't be happening."

Earl spat towards hernot that ghosts had spit, but he tried. "You're evil. You know she squashes snails, and she poisoned the neighbour's dog, Frankie. I can give you those details later if you like."

"We might not need them." I turned to Ethel. "He says you squash snails, and you poisoned the neighbour's dog, Frankie. You're a real piece of work. I can't wait to go to the police." I looked at Earl. "Look, I'm not getting very far, and I don't want to spend any more time here. She's horrible."

"This could all be an act for all I know."

Actually, I had a good idea. "Would you like to meet the poltergeist?"

Her eyes bugged open. "What?! You can't invite one of those into my house."

"I can do whatever I want. In the ghost world, I have clout." Who would've ever thought I'd be bragging to someone? I had an appointment in an hour for an interview with a man who made naked-looking products, so aprons with bare chests or boobs, and towels, T-shirts. The range was endless, and in such poor taste, so I wanted to wrap this up quickly. As far as I knew, Adam hadn't gone into the darkness or the light, but he owed me big time for solving his murder. "Adam. Hey, Adam, it's Avery."

He popped into existence next to Earl. They introduced themselves, and he looked at me. "What do you need? And does this mean I've paid you back?"

"I need you to break a couple of things just in there. Think you can manage it?"

"Yes. And the matter of my debt to you being gone?"

"Potentially. Break the things, and we'll see."

"What? Break what?" Ethel's eyes darted around the backyard as if she were trying to see the ghosts.

Because I'd invited him here, he could wander into the house, and he did. A pretty white vase with a floral pattern sat on the coffee table. Adam put his ghostly hand on it. He shut his eyes and concentrated. The vase started shaking. Then as Adam's force built, it rocked from side to side before falling to the floor and smashing.

"Nice work!" I was impressed, but only because he wasn't doing it to my things.

"Get that thing out of my house! I'll go. I'll go. I'll go right now. Just get him out."

"I want Earl freed right now, or my friend will stay here and break things for eternity."

Adam swore. "That wasn't the deal."

I rolled my eyes. "Seriously?"

Understanding dawned. To be fair, I hadn't explained the situation to him.

"Well?" I raised both eyebrows. "What's it going to be? A lifetime of hauntings and fraud charges, or hand yourself in, and at least you'll have peace and quiet in gaol?"

She gave herself a small smile, and in it I saw the victory she thought she would get. She assumed she could run away. "Okay, I'll free him. I'll need to get my things." She turned to go back into the house.

"Her things are in the shed."

"Thanks, Earl." I smiled. "Your things are in the shed." She stopped dead and turned back to me. I gave her a "come on, I wasn't born yesterday" look. "Earl told me."

She huffed and went into the shed. Shortly she came out with a feather, black candle, lavender oil, and a white crystal. She lit the candle and incanted some gibberish, walking in a circle around the backyard. When she was done, she put the candle on the ground in the middle of the yard. She placed the crystal on the ground. She dipped the feather in the lavender oil, then held it over the flame. She said something else as the feather flared with orange and blue flame. As the fire neared her fingers, she let the blackened feather fall to the ground. As soon as it hit, it was as if a heaviness lifted. I hadn't noticed it before, but it was obvious in its absence.

Earl blinked and became more solid. "I think it worked. Hang on." He walked to the back fence and through it. "Yippee! I'm free! I'm free."

I grinned, and tears moistened my eyes. "Yes! Have fun, Earl."

"Bye!"

And that was it. He was gone.

I looked at Ethel. "Thank you. He's left. Now, let's go to the police station. I'm driving."

"I can take myself."

"Ha, sure you can. Seriously, how stupid do you think I am?" I gave Adam a nod. He made his way to one of her framed photos on a side table, and it started rocking like the vase had.

She swallowed, and her hands shot up. "Okay, okay, I'll go. You can take me."

"You can stop now, Adam. But don't go anywhere yet."

He rolled his eyes. "This is kind of fun, but I have better things to do."

Yeah right. I didn't grace that with an answer. I looked at Ethel, and this time it appeared as though she realised she wasn't getting away with anything any longer. Her shoulders drooped, as did her face.

"Ready?"

She sighed. "I suppose so." I didn't miss the dirty look she gave me as we made our way back through her house.

Adam followed us to the front porch. After Ethel locked her front door for the last time, I gave him a nod. "You're free to go."

He gave me a mock bow. As he straightened, darkness shadowed the front garden. An oppressive sensation closed in on me. Adam's mouth dropped open, and his confusion turned to horror. "No. No, I'm not ready!" But he had no say.

A black hole opened at the front fence. He was sucked towards it. "No. Save me, Avery. Please!"

I gasped because it wasn't pretty. His form distorted until it was barely a caricature of a person. As horrible a human as he was, even I didn't enjoy his screams as he disappeared.

"First you want to hurry. Now you're dragging the chain. What are you staring at?" Ethel stood at the front fence, hand on hip, probably resigned to her fate. She didn't realise the other destiny that likely awaited her. I didn't have the heart to say anything. It was my job to make sure she paid her dues in this life. The next life was not my jurisdiction.

"Nothing, Ethel. Absolutely nothing."

If you enjoyed *A Frozen Stiff*, you might want to grab book 5. It will be out in the first half of 2023. Watch out for it on preorder. And if you're looking for more cosy mysteries and haven't tried my Paranormal Investigation Bureau series yet, why not grab *Witchnapped in Westerham*. It has over 3000 positive Goodreads ratings and reviews.

All it takes is one morning for Sydney Photographer Lily Bianchi's life to go off the rails and over a cliff.

A well-dressed English woman turns up at her door, swearing she's a witch. If that's not crazy enough, she explains Lily's brother, James, has been kidnapped and the Paranormal Investigation Bureau needs Lily's help finding him. And the craziest part? The Englishwoman tells Lily she's a witch too.

Before she can say, "Where's my coffee?" she's on a plane bound for Westerham, England. Unfortunately, England's not as welcoming as she hoped--she's barely arrived before she gets set up, arrested, and almost shot.

Things can only get better from here, right? Yeah, right...

ALSO BY DIONNE LISTER

Paranormal Investigation Bureau

Witchnapped in Westerham #1

Witch Swindled in Westerham #2

Witch Undercover in Westerham #3

Witchslapped in Westerham #4

Witch Silenced in Westerham #5

Killer Witch in Westerham #6

Witch Haunted in Westerham #7

Witch Oracle in Westerham #8

Witchbotched in Westerham #9

Witch Cursed in Westerham #10

Witch Heist in Westerham #11

Witch Burglar in Westerham #12

Vampire Witch in Westerham #13

Witch War in Westerham #14

Westerham Witches and a Venetian Vendetta #15

Witch Nemesis in Westerham #16

Witch Catastrophe in Westerham #17

Witch Karma in Westerham Book #18

Witch Showdown in Westerham Book #19 (coming November 2022)

Haunting Avery Winters

(Paranormal Cosy Mystery)

A Killer Welcome #1

A Regrettable Roast #2

A Fallow Grave #3

A Frozen Stiff #4

#5 (Out first half of 2023)

The Circle of Talia

(YA Epic Fantasy)

Shadows of the Realm

A Time of Darkness

Realm of Blood and Fire

The Rose of Nerine

(Epic Fantasy)

Tempering the Rose

Forging the Rose (Out September 2022)

ABOUT THE AUTHOR

USA Today bestselling author, Dionne Lister is a Sydneysider with a degree in creative writing, a love of storytelling, and two Siamese cats. Daydreaming has always been her passion, so writing was a natural progression from staring out the window in primary school, and being an author was a dream she held since childhood.

Unfortunately, writing was only a hobby while Dionne worked as a property valuer in Sydney, until her mid-thirties when she returned to study and completed her creative writing degree. Since then, she has indulged her passion for writing while raising two children with her husband. Her books have attracted praise from Apple iBooks and have reached #1 on Amazon and iBooks charts worldwide, frequently occupying top 100 lists in fantasy and mystery.

Printed in Great Britain
by Amazon